Falcon Quinn

and the Bullies of Greenblud

Jennifer Finney Boylan

By the same author:

Falcon Quinn and the Black Mirror

Falcon Quinn and the Crimson Vapor

Falcon Quinn

and the Bullies of Greenblud

I.

Up in the Air

The Zeppelin drifted gently above the Berkshire Mountains, bearing its crew of mysterious creatures. Standing on the observation deck at the back of the blimp, Falcon Quinn's wings fluttered in the summer breeze. Everything was quiet in the world below.

"Dude," said Max, a Sasquatch, coming outside from the Zeppelin snack bar. "I got ya some cocoa."

Falcon folded his wings so they lay flat across his back. "Thanks, Max." He held the styrofoam cup of hot chocolate in his hands, and the warmth spread through his fingers. It felt good.

Max looked out over the horizon. "This is so awesome! Us up in the clouds! Our lives——" He paused mid-sentence to raise the cocoa to his lips, and then shoved the whole thing, cup and all, into his mouth. Hot chocolate dripped down his Bigfoot face. "—are unbelievably, amazingly great!" Then he roared. The sound of Max's jubilation echoed on the green hills beneath them.

"Who's doing all that shouting?" said Merideath, a prissy vampire. "As if I didn't know."

"I'm drinkin' hot cocoa!" shouted Max, in ecstasy. "You should have some too! It's amazing!"

Merideath, dressed in black, rolled her eyes. "Cocoa isn't what I want to drink."

"Bite me," said Max.

"I'd like to," said Merideath.

"Guys," said Falcon. The halo that shone around his head glowed blue. "Let's not fight."

"Sorry, angel-face," said Merideath. "I'd hate to upset you. Who know, maybe you'd wind up scorching me with your laser-beam eye thing."

"I'm not using that any more," said Falcon.

"Pity," said Merideath.

"Unless he has to, man," said Max. "Unless a situation calls for totally drastic measures."

Sparkbolt, a young Frankenstein, lurched out onto the observation deck. "Rrrr," he said.

"Hey, Sparky!" shouted Max. "You want some cocoa? We got donuts too."

"Donuts bad," said Sparkbolt.

"No, no," said Max. "Donuts good."

Sparkbolt thought it over, then took a bite of one of the donuts that lay upon a golden platter. Powdered sugar coated the Frankenstein's lips. Sparkbolt looked at Falcon Quinn. "Friend," he said.

"I swear to god," said Merideath. "Being with him is like being with a three year old."

"Yeah, dude," said Max. "A totally awesome, giant three year old who can rip peoples arms out of their sockets."

"Rrr," said Sparkbolt.

Mrs. Redflint, the Dragon Lady, came outside to join them. She was the Dean of Students, back at the Academy for Monsters. Their school, on an island in the Bermuda Triangle, was hundreds of miles behind them now. They'd left the island at dawn the day before.

"Young people," she said. "I must insist that you stop making this disturbance. Our cloaking device hides the Zeppelin from the eyes of humans. But they can still hear one's voice, if one is so careless as to indulge in needless roaring!"

"It wasn't needless, Mrs. R," said Max. "I was totally grooving on some hot chocolate! It's got these awesome mini-marshmallows in it! They make me happy! Whoo, yeah!" He roared again.

"Maximillian," said Mrs. Redflint. A small spurt of crimson flame shot out of her mouth. "Go inside this instant. And consider the consequences of your actions."

"Okay, okay," said Max, walking toward the door. "I'll consider the consequences of my enjoying this awesome cocoa, is what I'll do."

Mrs. Redflint watched him go. "Honestly, I don't know what I'm going to do about that boy."

"He's not going to like being turned into a human," said Falcon.

"Ugh," said Merideath. "Don't talk about it. It's like a stake in my heart."

"I don't expect any of you to like it," said Mrs. Redflint. "But it is the mission you have accepted. There is very important work to be done. Lives are at stake!" Merideath cringed. "That is, lives are— in the balance."

Megan Crofton, a wind elemental, came onto the deck along with her friends, Destynee the enchanted slug and Weems, the ghoul. Behind them was Johnny Frankenstein, the boy who could play an electric guitar plugged into his own neck. Johnny didn't look well.

"We heard a noise," said Megan. Her long black hair blew around her neck. Falcon couldn't tell if this was from the breezes swirling around the Zeppelin, or if Megan was simply generating her own gusts. She did that sometimes when she was worried, and she'd been worried a lot of late. Ever since she'd been diagnosed as a wind elemental, she'd been slowly fading.

"It was your idiot friend," said Merideath. "The orangutan. To him, a cup of cocoa is like beef Wellington."

"We do not insult our fellow students," said Mrs. Redflint. A little smoke came out her nose. "Unless necessary."

"Rrr," said Sparkbolt, and picked Merideath up by the neck, lifting her off her feet. "Sasquatch friend Sparkbolt. Sasquatch good. Vampire, bad!"

"Put me down, Lugbolt!" said Merideath. "Don't touch my person!"

"Oh, for heaven's sakes," said Mrs. Redflint. She blew a sudden cloud of red flame at Sparkbolt. He dropped Merideath onto the floor.

"Fire BAD!" shouted Sparkbolt. "BAD!"

"You're okay," said Johnny Frankenstein, coming over to Sparkbolt. "It's gone now." He put his hand on Sparkbolts' shoulder. For a moment the two Frankensteins stood like that together.

"Friend," said Sparkbolt.

"Yes," said Jonny, in a faint voice. "I'm your friend. We're all your friends. Even Merideath."

"He tried to choke me!" whined Merideath. "He tried to kill me!"

"Well, he didn't. So I guess you're okay," said Destynee, the giant enchanted slug.

"Yeah, sluggo," said Merideath. "But maybe I'll take your advice with a grain of salt."

"We're all okay," said Falcon Quinn. His halo was still glowing. "We're going to be fine."

"Indeed," said Mrs. Redflint, looking at the young monsters. "You are all in perfect health." Johnny Frankenstein got back to his feet, and coughed. "And if you cannot focus on the task at hand instead of your own disagreements, then this mission is doomed. Do you hear me? I say doomed." She shot a big cloud of red flame from her mouth.

"This mission of ours," said Weems. "Can it tell us more of the details? The crispy delicious minutiae of it all? Yes? Yes?" Weems was a small, completely bald boy, with jagged teeth. He was wearing tattered black rags, from his shoulders to his feet. He rubbed his hands together.

"When we land," said Mrs. Redflint. "It won't be long now."

"Jonny?" said Destynee. "Are you okay? You look a little pale."

Jonny coughed into his fist again. "I'm okay," he said.

"I hate it when you are sick," said Destynee.

"And I hate it," said Weems, "When you hate that he is sick!" His eyes glowed. "I am, at all times, concerned with the Beloved!"

Destynee sighed and rolled her eyes. "Don't call me that," she said. "It's creepy."

"Yes, yes!" said Weems. "It is!"

Ank-hoptet, the mummy, walked onto the deck, bandages trailing from her gauze mini-dress. "I have come to dwell among you!" she said importantly.

"Be still my heart," said Merideath.

"There," said Mrs. Redflint, pointing toward the horizon. A dilapidated barn stood at the edge of a corn field.

"Is this our new dwelling?" asked Ank-hoptet. "Is this the new realm where I shall rule?"

"It doesn't look like a high school," said Megan, her voice rising. "It doesn't look like a school at all!"

"It's not a school," said Mrs. Redflint.

A silo stood next to the barn. Hundreds of bats flew out of it.

"It's a safe house."

"It looks so homey," said Weems. "A place one might settle." He looked at Destynee with longing once more. "With one's Beloved. A place where one might eat one's scrumptious children!"

"Not listening," said Destynee.

"Mrs. Redflint?" said Falcon Quinn. "Is this where you're going to do it?"

"Do what, man?" said Max, coming back on to the deck. He had a banana in his hand.

"The place they're going to turn us into humans," said Megan. Tears glimmered in her eyes.

"Ugh," said Merideath. "It's so disgusting."

"It's just for a little while, though, right?" said Destynee. "You said it was just until we completed our mission?"

"Indeed," said Mrs. Redflint.

"And you'll tell us about this mission—" said Jonny Frankenstein.

"Soon," said Mrs. Redflint.

"I'm scared," said Megan. She flickered in and out of sight for a moment. For an instant, Falcon feared she was going to go completely invisible again.

"Rrrr," said Sparkbolt. "Human bad."

"We're all going to be all right," said Falcon, turning to his friends. "As long as we stick together."

"And so we shall!" shouted a voice. Pearl, the Chupakabra, came buzzing out onto the deck on her tiny wings. "For we are pledged, together! As friends! I have pledged to all my deadly stinger! And my life! For I am—La CHUPAKABRA! THE FAMOUS GOATSUCKER OF PERU!"

"Sssh," said Mrs. Redflint. "We're coming in for a landing now."

They stood together in a semicircle, watching the Earth approach as the Zeppelin descended. To the far left was Max, eating his banana; Pearl the Chupakabra buzzed above his right shoulder. Next to Max was Megan Crofton, her hair blowing around her, and next to Megan was Ank-hoptet, the Egyptian. The two Frankensteins, Sparkbolt and Jonny, stood together in the middle, with Merideath standing at Jonny's left. Destynee the enchanted slug was next to Jonny, and Weems was next to Destynee, his Beloved. In the center of the group was Falcon Quinn, the angel. His halo faded as they drew nearer to the ground.

Falcon felt his two hearts pounding in his chest as they landed in the cornfield. Before him two grown-ups stood watching them, a man and a woman.

"Welcome," said the woman, whose name was Vega, former queen of the monster-slayers called The Guardians.

"Welcome," said the man, a huge, winged creature called The Crow.

Everything was suddenly very quiet. The Zeppelin settled into the cornfield.

"Hi Mom," said Falcon. "Hi Dad."

2.

A Failed Experiment

The old man descended the stairs to his laboratory in the basement chamber. He didn't come down here very much any more. Still, it was very much as he'd left it on that last terrible day— the long table with the leather straps, the table full of broken beakers, the electronic dynamo with its thick black cables running from here all the way up to the lightning rod on top of the castle's highest tower. He remembered how the building had shaken, as electricity had crackled from the skies and into this chamber, how his creation's fingers had twitched as it surged out of nothingness and into life.

The doctor felt something crunch beneath his feet, and he bent down to see what this might be. There, warped by what had been the intense heat of the fire on the last day, was a guitar pick.

"My boy," said the doctor, looking around the lab again, the guitar pick clenched in his fist. "My... boys." He raised his fist into the air, and shook it. Then the man crumpled, overcome by grief. The guitar pick slipped out of his hand and fell to the floor. The doctor put his hand on his forehead and covered his eyes. After a moment, he began to shake softly.

"Come now, it's not that bad," said a voice. The doctor looked up and saw a man wearing a tweed jacket standing at the top of his basement stairs. He had a luxurious yellow beard and twinkling eyes.

"No one's allowed in here!" shouted the doctor. "No one!"

"You're in here," the stranger pointed out.

"This is my laboratory!" shouted the doctor. "My private sanctum!"

"But what a mess you've made of the place!" said the stranger. "What happened? Was there a fire?"

"I'll call the police, yes I will," said the doctor. "You're trespassing! This is private property!"

"Come, now, doctor," said the man with the beard. "We both know you won't do that. The publicity. The scandal!"

"Who are you!" said the doctor. "What do you want?"

"I am Mr. Lyons," said the stranger. "And I want many things."

"Are you from the university?" said the doctor. "You tell them I'm never going back! That place! Where they.. they laughed at my experiments!"

"I am not from there," said Mr. Lyons. In his hands he held a book. "I am.. a librarian."

"A librarian?" said the doctor. "I've never heard of a librarian that makes house calls. No, I have not."

"Doctor," said Mr. Lyons. "I have come about...the boys."

"My sons," said the doctor, and his voice choked. "I am so...sorry. For what I did."

"What did you do?" asked Mr. Lyons.

"I.. I turned my back on them."

"Yes," said Mr. Lyons. "Yes you did."

"I was so angry," said the doctor. "I wanted them to be… like me. Instead of…"

"Instead of like themselves," said Mr. Lyons. He made a deep rumbling purring sound in his throat. "Yes. It is a very common thing. You shouldn't be so hard on yourself, Dr. Frankenstein. It is very hard, to let the little ones free."

"Don't you see?" said the doctor. "Because of me… my sons wander the earth. Without love, without hope, without knowledge even of who they are! They are lost to me, yes they are! Because of my blindness!"

Mr. Lyons came down the stairs and put a book in the mans hand. It was a beautiful book, with gilt-edged pages and a leather cover. "My friend," he said. "They are not lost."

3.

The Fire Barn

"Whoa, whoa, whoa," said Max. "I signed up to help people. I didn't volunteer to get—"

"Destroyed?" said Falcon's mother, Vega. She was a beautiful but worn looking woman, dressed all in white. When last she'd encountered Max, she had transformed him into a page of sheet music, a metamorphosis that Falcon himself had finally undone by playing the piece upon the Godzooka, an enormous kind of tuba made out of intestines that took up a large corner of the gymnasium back on Monster Island.

"And so!" shouted Pearl. "Our enemy has survived! We shall engage her in battle! We shall prepare to die unto the death!"

Mrs. Redfliint spat a column of fire in Pearl and Max's direction. "Enough," she said. "All will be explained. You are in no danger." She cast a glance at The Crow. "Or so I have been given to understand."

"You are all here under my protection," said The Crow grimly. "The Guardian Queen has come to see the error of her ways."

"Is that true, Mom?" said Falcon. "You're not trying to kill us any more?"

Vega kneeled down before her son. "No, Falcon," she said. "I am not trying to kill you." She looked at the other assembled monsters. "Any of you."

"Well, I think that's refreshing!" said a voice from behind them. This was Mr. Hake, the Vice Principal of the Academy for Monsters, wearing a kind of admiral's uniform, and with a long aviator's scarf tied around his neck. "Yes, refreshing!"

"I take it your passage from Monster Island to this place was unencumbered by needless drama," said The Crow.

"Flying a Zeppelin is fun," said Mr. Hake. "It's nice to go up in the air! Up in the sky so blue!." He was, when he wasn't being annoyingly pleasant, the Terrible Kraken. "But I like the ground, too. It's so squishy!"

"Dude," Max said to the Crow. "When you said, 'this place,' where did you mean?"

"Indeed!" shouted Pearl. "What is this place that we have arrived, and what danger now awaits us here? We shall draw our swords if necessary, and fight off all of those who would oppose us!"

"I know where we are," said Ankh-hoptet. "We have arrived at last at my kingdom. The place where I shall rule!"

"Oh," said Merideath. "Then we must be in Toilet Town!"

"This," growled the mummy, "is not the name by which my kingdom is known!"

"Toilet Town," said Max, laughing. "Dude! She said the mummy's kingdom is called—"

"I heard her," said Megan, and a gust of cold wind blew from her. "I don't think that's the name of this place." She looked at the green mountains surrounding them. "I don't think this is your empire, either, Ankh-hoptet. Sorry."

"Indeed," said The Crow. "This place is known as— New Hampshire!"

"Ugh," said Merideath. "I was right the first time."

"Why are we here?" whined Destynee. "What are we supposed to do?"

"Careful, my Beloved," said Weems. "It mustn't cry its tears again. The salt! It presents a threat to the perfection of the skin!"

"Shut up," said Destynee, whose skin indeed was dissolving beneath the trails of the enchanted slug's salt tears. "Don't call me that!" She turned to Jonny Frankenstein "Jonny, tell him not to call me that. It's creepy."

"Indeed," said Weems, cackling through his yellow, triangular teeth. "It is!"

"Knock it off, Weems," said Jonny Frankenstein. "Don't make me jolt you with my lightning bolts."

"I love your lightning bolts," said Merideath. "I love everything about you!"

"Enough!" shouted Mrs. Redflint. "Come, children! Let us assemble in the assembling-place. And we shall explain the task that lies before you!"

"Yes," said Vega. She looked mournful. "We will explain it all."

"This way," said The Crow, urging them forward into a barn that stood at the edge of the clearing. One side of it appeared to have, at some point, been on fire. The northern wall consisted of a series of logs, all charred black. "All will be made clear."

As the young monsters filed into the barn, Mr. Hake remained behind. "I'm going to make sure the blimp is okay!" he said. A moment later, he transformed into the Terrible Kraken, and his tentacles flopped out in every direction.

"Dude," said Max.

"Come along, children," said Vega. "Into the barn you go."

Given his mother's enthusiasm for shepherding them all into the old building, Falcon half expected some trick, as if once inside, the floor would open and they would all be cast into a pit of glue. Instead, the barn contained only bales of hay. A horse looked over at them from a stall.

"This is the Fire Barn," said The Crow. "It is here where we will do what must be done to you."

"You said you needed us to be disguised for this— mission?" said Falcon. "You said you needed for people to think we were— human?"

"Yes, yes, yes," said Mrs. Redflint. "But please. Let us start at the beginning."

"The beginning," said The Crow. "Yessss. We should begin at the beginning…" His long black wings fluttered for a moment, as he thought. "Well, I suppose it begins with the war between monsters and guardians. The war which has only recently come to a conclusion."

"Yes!" Pearl shouted. "The war which we have won! By defeating the Guardians upon the terrible field of battle!"

"The war was won on the battlefield at Monster Island, yes," said The Crow. "But it has been won in other places as well. Including— ah—-" He looked at Vega uncertainly.

"Including in my heart," said Vega.

"Aw," said Merideath.

"Laugh if you wish," said Vega. "I do not expect to find sympathy from those whose lives I threatened, for so many years."

"I have forgiven her," said The Crow. "I hope that you will forgive her in time, as well."

"You killed a lot of our friends," said Jonny Frankenstein, his face dark. "Monsters we'll never see again."

"And there are many Guardians who will also never walk the earth," said Vega. "Can you bring them back?" Jonny fell silent, although his eyes still flickered angrily. "Even Falcon, with his healing eye, cannot restore all our losses."

"But there are some who are still lost," said The Crow. "Monsters who were sent into hiding. It is these souls whom we have brought you here to save."

"Hiding?" said Falcon. "Who's in hiding?"

"Five monsters," said Vega. "Were captured as children by one of our guardian ships. We intended to destroy them, as we destroyed all young monsters in those days." She sounded proud.

There was a moment of silence as Vega seemed to think back with nostalgia upon the days of murder and destruction. She sighed.

"But then they escaped. At night they stole one of the lifeboats, and lowered it into the sea. We pursued them swiftly when the betrayal was discovered. And followed them here, to this town."

"I am not certain that 'betrayal's' the best word to describe the actions of young people," said the Crow. "who were but trying to save their own lives."

"No?" said Vega. She laughed bitterly. "Ah, no. Of course not. They were so noble, these brave young monsters. These five."

"What happened to them?" said Falcon. He felt his two hearts beating rapidly in his chest, as if he could imagine what it must have been like for those five young monsters to run for their lives, with a guardian army behind them.

"They found their way here," said the Crow.

"But—where's here?" said Megan. "What is this place?"

"It is an Outpost," said Crow. "One of many in the human world, from which we observe the progress of their so-called civilization."

"You spied on us, too, darling," said Vega icily. "Back before we buried the hatchet. You did a lot of spying."

"As was necessary," said the Crow. "To protect our lives."

"What happened when these monsters got here?" asked Falcon.

"They were disguised," said the Crow. "We ran them through a Bland-a-tron."

"Rrr," moaned Sparkbolt. "Bland-a-tron bad."

"But this was no ordinary Bland-a-tron," said the Crow. "These monsters were not only transformed into beings that looked like humans. Their memories were altered, so that they had no awareness of their own true natures. So that they could be hidden, here, in this town in New Hampshire, safe from Guardian attack."

"Which they were," said Vega. "We were right behind them. Only moments after those children were whisked out of this barn, my Guardians attacked! We burned this barn, and killed the monsters who had manned the controls of the Bland-a-tron. A zombie, I believe, and two Banshees."

"You shall pay for the lives you have taken!" shouted Pearl, buzzing close to Vega, her stinger extended. "You shall suffer the same pain you brought to the innocent! There will be blood tonight!"

"Pearl," said The Crow. "Please. The Monsters and the Guardians are now at peace. There will be no more bloodshed."

"I live for the shedding of blood!" shouted Pearl. "In the name of justice, and all those who have no champion of their own! I am— la Chupakabra! The famous goatsucker of Peru!"

"Oh my god," said Meredith, rolling her eyes. "Here we go again."

"Pearl," said the Crow. "Your courage is needed. But we need you to be brave not in order to spill blood. But to help us find the five missing monsters."

"Missing?" said Falcon. "What do you mean, missing?"

There was an awkward silence for a moment. Then Mrs. Redflint stepped forward. "The only ones who knew the identities of the disguised monsters were the three who helped transform them. The three who were killed in the Guardian attack."

"So wait, what?" said Max. "Those other monsters—"

"Are now approaching their thirteenth birthdays," said The Crow. "And their monster natures will begin to emerge."

"Which will put them all in terrible danger," said Mrs. Redflint.

"Wait, where are they now?" said Falcon. "They're not just— wandering the countryside?"

"No," said the Crow. "They are all freshman. At Greenblud High."

"At—where?"

"A private boarding school," said Mrs. Redflint. "It's very exclusive!"

"People are just dying to get in," said Weems. "Ha-ha! Ha-ha!"

"Ugh," said Merideath. "Sometimes I want to bite my own neck."

"This is all totally Wack-a-mole," said Max. "Why don't you just scoop 'em up. Call out Olly olly oxen-free?"

"I do not understand this Oxenfree. What does this mean?"

"Dude, it's a saying. It's like you just tell everybody game's over, come on home!"

"But don't you see," said Mrs. Redflint impatiently. She stamped one foot, and a big burst of flame issued from her nostrils. "These monsters do not know who they are. They think they are humans. We have given them false memories of their own happy childhoods. They are disguised, even from themselves!"

"Whoa," said Max. "This is totally blowing my mind."

"And when their monster natures begin to develop," said The Crow. "They will be in considerable danger."

"I should think that it is these humans who will be in danger!" shouted Pearl. "That they shall soon find themselves in the presence of mighty fighters, of courage and daring!"

"Perhaps at first," said Vega. "But I can tell you the humans will be merciless once they realize these students are different. They will be tortured. Humiliated. Put in prisons. Hospitals. Humans are like that, you know."

"They're worse than you are," said Merideath. "Were, I mean."

"The threat is more profound than that," said The Crow. "Once the humans learn that monsters are real, our whole world will be endangered. We have been protected, all these centuries, by our stealth. But word will spread that monsters walk the earth. A war will come, a war that will make the battle against the Guardians seem tame."

"Well all right," said Falcon. "What do we have to do? We're in, right?" He looked at the others.

"We shall bring our swords and stingers to this challenge!" shouted Pearl. "We shall risk all to defend our comrades!"

"Yeah," said Max. He roared his deep Sasquatch roar. "I'm in."

"Me too," said Megan.

"We're all in," said Jonny Frankenstein. "Aren't we?" The young monsters all shouted their assent, except for Merideath, who stood with her arms crossed.

"Okay, fine," she said, rolling her eyes.

"Then it's all decided," said Mrs. Redflint. She pulled on a handle on the floor, revealing a trapdoor and a long set of stairs that led underground. "In the basement of this complex is a Bland-a-tron. It will transform you into humans for ninety-nine days. You have three months to find the hidden monsters, and bring them back here to Mr. Swishtail. He will arrange for your transportation back to Monster Academy.

"Mr. Swishtail?" said Falcon. "Who's that?"

"Oh, I'm sorry," said Mrs. Redflint, turning toward the horse, chewing hay in the corner. "Mr. Swishtail is director of our field program. You're looking forward to helping our brave young monsters along aren't you?"

"Nay," said the horse, chewing.

"Dude," said Max. "An enchanted horse!"

"Nay," said Mr. Swishtail.

"You're not an enchanted horse?" said Max.

"Nay," said Mr. Swishtail.

"Mr. Swishtail is an enchanted pony," said Mrs. Redflint.

Mr. Swishtail nattered in his stall, then sighed.

"Dude," said Max. "Why the long face?"

"All right then," said Mrs. Redflint. "Shall we begin?"

She stood by the trapdoor, and gestured toward the descending stairs with one of her scaly hands. "Through this portal lies your greatest challenge yet. You have battled guardians, dueled with enemies, fought off attacks on land and sea. But now you embark upon the most terrible ordeal of all."

She looked them all in the eyes, and Falcon thought he almost detected a short flicker of fear in their depths.

"Ninth grade," she said, and all the monsters screamed.

4.

Wagon Wheel

It was late in the day, and Falcon and his friends were now riding in a small bus through the White Mountains of New Hampshire. Mrs. Redflint, behind the wheel, cast a glance back at her passengers in the rearview mirror, and shuddered. The monsters all looked much more frightening now that that they had all been transformed into humans.

Considering the drama of the change before them, there had been little resistance as the young monsters had stepped into the Bland-a-tron. They had come out the other side with their monster natures hidden, a process that was more dramatic in some cases than others. Merideath, for instance, looked exactly the same, except that her fangs had shrunk back to the size of so-called "normal" canine teeth. Johnny Frankenstein and Sparkbolt also looked largely the same, except that the bolts on their necks were gone.

Mrs. Redflint jammed on the brakes as a large bull moose lumbered across the road before them. It paused at the side of the road to give the bus a dirty look.

"Rrr," said Sparkbolt. "Moose bad."

"You're going to have to start using verbs," said Merideath.

"Verbs bad," said Sparkbolt.

"Verbs are bad," said Merideath.

"Rrr," said Sparkbolt.

"It is true!" shouted Pearl. "Henceforward you must speak in a manner less distinctive! Thus will our secret identities be preserved! And our comrades returned to us unharmed!"

"We are so dead," said Max. His transformation had been one of the more dramatic ones. No longer did he look like a giant ape. Now he had a big ponytail and a beard. He wore a t-shirt that said: GRATEFUL DEAD.

"We shall be protected!" said Pearl. "By our loyalty to one another! None shall attack my brothers and survive!" Her changes had been dramatic as well. Instead of a flying creature with a long stinger, now she was a teenage girl with an iPod and knee-high leather boots. Her fingernails were long, and painted black.

"We'll be all right," said Megan, and glanced over at Falcon. "Won't we?" But Falcon didn't respond. He just stared out the window at the White Mountains. "Falcon?"

"What?" he said. Falcon no longer had wings, or a halo. He seemed a little glum.

"You okay?" said Megan. She reached out and took his hand, and squeezed it.

"I'm all right," said Falcon. "I just— I don't see why they couldn't have let me know they were all right."

Megan nodded. "Your parents, you mean. The Crow, and Vega."

"Yeah," said Falcon. "Them."

"Didn't your father say he was nursing Vega back to health?"

"Yeah, he said that. I guess she's fine now, and isn't trying to kill us any more. I mean, you know. Awesome."

"It's good that she's not trying to kill us," said Megan.

"I know. But they're already onto this whole new thing, rescuing these missing monsters. And we all volunteered to help."

"Do you wish we hadn't volunteered?" said Megan.

"No, it's fine. I just wish they'd stop once for five minutes, though, and—"

"And tell you what they feel," said Megan. She nodded. "Well, don't be too sad, Falcon. My mother always let me know how she felt. How much more she cared about my sisters than me. Maybe you're lucky, not knowing."

"Maybe," said Falcon.

"We're almost there," said Mrs. Redflint. "Now remember what we told you. You're all new at Greenblud this fall. You don't know each other. Anyone asks, you just say you all took the same bus together from the airport."

"Which is almost true," said Max. "Except it wasn't an airport, man, it was a Zepplin-port!"

"Yes," said Mrs. Redflint. "Thank you for that Maximillian. Your mission is to fit quietly in to life at Greenblud High, and to find the missing monsters."

"Yeah, about that," said Jonny Frankenstein.

"Yes, Jonathan?"

"How do we do that, exactly? If these monsters have been disguised, and even they don't even know who they are—? How are we supposed to know who's who? You know a lot of ninth graders seem like monsters."

"Ah," said Mrs. Redflint. "Well, we believe that the four missing monsters are most likely creatures like yourselves. We suspect that they will detect the monster in you, and be drawn to you."

"Drawn to us?" said Merideath. "Like bears to honey, you mean?"

"Each of us seeks our own kind," said Mrs. Redflint. "Even if we do not know what our own kind might be. Sometimes we are better, at first, at detecting that in others than in ourselves." She looked concerned. "But you must all be careful. You are strong monsters now, and the effects of the Bland-a-tron can me erased if you get overly excited, or experience intense emotions. If that happens, you will revert to your monster form like that, and our mission—indeed, your very lives—will be in danger."

"Don't worry, Mrs. R," said Max. "We'll be totally, totally mellow!" He roared.

"Oh dear," said Mrs. Redflint.

"Wait," said Jonny. "You said four monsters just now. Originally you said there were five."

"There were," said Mrs. Redflint, as they turned down a long driveway. A sign on an archway read: THE GREENBLUD SCHOOL. "One of them died. A frost worm."

"Dude," said Max.

"How was it killed?" said Weems, excited. "Strangled? Impaled?"

"I'm glad you're amused, Mr. Weems," said Mrs. Redflint. "But I'm afraid this young monster killed himself."

"What?" said Max. "Seriously? Why would anyone do that? When everything is so awesome!"

"He was driven to it," said Mrs. Redflint. "He did it because he could bear it no longer."

"Bear what no longer?" said Jonny.

"The bullies of Greenblud," said Mrs. Redflint, as they pulled up in front of a tall, Victorian mansion.

•

Falcon found his dorm room empty. The new arrivals had been divided up and sent off to find their new chambers. He had been put in a double room on a hall with a dozen or so other young men, many of whom were even now putting posters on their walls, and blasting music from their speakers. Falcon put his two suitcases on his bed, and sat down on the mattress. Across from him was an identical bed, unoccupied.

For the moment, he was alone. It was the first time Falcon had gotten a chance to catch his breath since they'd left the Academy for

Monsters days before. There was a lot to take in – the long journey across the ocean by Zeppelin, the mysterious mission they'd been given.

But nothing was as unsettling as the unexpected appearance of his parents at the landing field. He had last seen them at the haunted windmill on the island of the Guardians. His mother and his father had engaged in a furious battle, while he and his friends had rescued Megan from the entangling sails of the windmill. In the end, his father had summoned hundreds of birds— carrion crows and jackdaws—and they had descended upon Vega with their talons. The last he'd seen of his parents, the Crow was flying toward the horizon with his mother's bloodied body in his arms.

A few weeks later, Falcon had been mortally wounded during the battle of Monster Island. In what he'd thought were his dying moments, Falcon had found himself dreaming he was on the Island of Nightmares, with the Shepard of Dreams, The Watcher, whom Falcon had known as the school librarian, Mr. Lyons. The man had given Falcon reason to hope that his parents had been saved, and that he would see them again. But everything in his dream was strangely bright and clear, more real than reality. Mr. Lyons, he'd asked. Are we dead?

Dead, said the librarian. For heavens sakes, Falcon, why would you think you were dead? On such a day as this?

They stabbed me, Mr. Lyons And I think you must be dead too. We both are.

Falcon Quinn, said Mr. Lyons. No man can kill me.

Falcon had looked around at the roaring ocean, the strange cloud filled sky. Why not? There's some law that you can't kill a librarian?

There should be, said Mr. Lyons. That is a law I would surely endorse.

Later, The Watcher had caught a salmon on a hook, and thrown it back into the sea. Mr. Lyons, he'd asked. Am I going to be all right?

Mr. Lyons looked thoughtful. I am not sure you mean by that, Falcon. You will have occasion for great joy, I think, and others of sadness and pain. You will find many things you are searching for and lose others. You will be surrounded by the voices of those who love you, and on other occasions find yourself stranded and alone. You will know great hunger and thirst; and then days will come when the table before you is piled high with warm bread and sweet butter. Above all, dear boy, you will have many choices to make. Perhaps with love, and humor, and the counsel of your friends you will make more right choices than wrong ones. So. If this is what you mean, then I suppose you will be alright, Falcon. Yes. You will be just fine.

After that, Falcon had faded out of the strange dream – if dream it was – and returned to the battlefield. When all was done, after the guardians and the monsters had at last made their tentative peace, what he'd been left with above all were those two images: one of his father flying away with his mother in his arms, and the other of the kindly, mysterious Watcher, encouraging him to believe in the goodness of his life.

Falcon didn't believe in his own goodness, and had even come to a kind of peace with the dual nature of his soul; he was a combination of his father's and his mother's views of the world. To be an angel meant being a monster in some ways, as well as the opposite of one— to be something that was decidedly not human, but just as decidedly not a creature of darkness. He was both monster, and non-monster; human and inhuman. It made him different from everyone else, which was a hard fate to bear. But he'd come to accept, even to be proud of his uniqueness. There were still times when Falcon felt a sense of sadness, as he considered that there was no one else in the world exactly like himself. But in recent days he'd come to see this as a kind of strength as well. It was just as The Watcher had told him: that in time he would understand that what he'd thought was his greatest curse was actually his great gift.

What he had not expected was that his parents, when they re-entered his life, would seem so aloof, so uninterested in him. Vega and the Crow had hardly said a word to him on the landing field— at least, no words to him that they had not spoken to all of the monsters. What had happened to them after The Crow flew off with Vega in his arms? After all the years of separation, were they together again? A couple?

When he was growing up in Cold River, Maine, he had longed for his parents to come back to him. He had dreamed of the three of them being a family again. Now, after all this time, it looked as if his mom and dad were together once more. But why didn't they want him? Were they really so selfish, to be more interested in each other than in their own son?

Falcon opened up his duffle bags and put his clothes into the built-in dresser in the dorm room's wall. He hung up his shirts, put his shoes on the floor, pulled the fitted sheets onto the bed and pillowcase onto his pillow. It didn't take long. As he finished unpacking, he caught a glimpse of himself in the mirror. For a second, he thought he was looking at a stranger. But the last year at the Academy for Monsters —not to mention the simple passage of time— had changed him. A lot had happened.

The Bland-a-tron had transformed him as well, of course, removing the outward signs of his monstrosity and leaving him looking more like a fourteen year old human. His wings were gone, along with his halo. But interestingly, he still had one blue eye, and one black one. His eyes had lost their power, for now; no longer could he shoot fireballs out of his black eye, or heal things with the blue one. But they still made him look a little strange, he thought. He feared that people would make fun of his eyes, that they would tease him about this difference. But then, who knew? Maybe this was another difference that strangers might discern as a strength.

"Hey, are you Falcon Quinn?" said a voice, and he turned. There in the doorway stood a boy about Falcon's height, with curling brown hair. He had one black eye and one green eye.

"Hi," said the boy. "I'm Malcolm."

•

Over in Max's dorm room, the Sasquatch-in-disguise was putting his clothes in a dresser when a boy with red hair knocked on the door. "Is this the right room?" he asked.

"Hey man," said Max. "Every room's the right room for something! Depends what you're looking for! If what you're looking for is Party-town, you've come to the right place! My name is Max! I play ultimate frisbee! I like eating pizzas! Everything is AWESOME!" He threw his head back and roared.

The red-haired boy looked terrified. He looked at the number on the door, and then at some papers in his hand.

"Hey, sorry," said Max. "I had something in my throat."

The red haired boy looked at the door again. He stepped into the room, holding an old-fashioned, beat-up suitcase in one hand. "I guess we're—"

"Room-mates, dude!" said Max. "We are going to PARTY!"

"Oh, I don't know if I'm allowed to party," said the boy. "I'm on a special diet."

"Well," said Max. "That's awesome! We'll party around your diet."

The boy put the suitcase on one of the beds. "Okay," he said, unconvinced. He sat down on the bare mattress and put his face in his hands.

"Hey," said Max. "You okay?"

The boy nodded, but tears quivered in his eyes. As Max watched, they brimmed over his eyelashes, and spilled down his cheeks.

"Hey, hey, hey," said Max. "Don't be. Aw." He looked around in panic. Then he went over to his bureau and got a chocolate bar out of his top drawer.

"Dude," said Max, sitting down next to the red-haired boy. "Have a Chunky."

The boy looked at Max, not comprehending. "What?"

"Have a Chunky bar. I love'em." He put the candy bar in the boy's hands. "Whatever's wrong with ya, a Chunky can cure. And whatever's NOT wrong with ya, a Chunky will prevent."

The boy held the candy bar in his hand. "Thank you," he said. He looked at Max. "You're very large."

"Well yeah," said Max. "I like jumpin' up and down! Best thing you can be, is bouncy."

"Oh I'm not bouncy," said the boy.

"Not yet, man," said Max. He put out his hand. "I'm Max. What's your name?"

"I'm Milton," said the boy, and he took a bite of Chunky.

"There ya go," said Max. "Down the hatch!"

"Hey," said Milton. "It's good."

•

"Do you like The Cupcakes?" asked Muffy Chicago. She was tacking a poster of a band to the wall in their dorm room.

"What cupcakes?" said Megan.

Muffy looked at Megan as if she could not quite believe what she had heard. "The Cupcakes?" she said. She nodded toward the poster, which showed a group of four very fashionable young women holding guitars and drumsticks. "Oh my god I think they are a-may-zing."

"I don't really know their music," said Megan.

Muffy looked at Megan as if she had been personally insulted. "How is that even possible?" said Muffy. She opened up her duffle bag and removed a very large bag of cosmetics, then took this over to the dresser and dumped it all into the top drawer. Then she went back to her duffle and filled the rest of the drawers as well. She looked back at Megan. "I'm sorry, do you want me to save one drawer for you?"

Megan felt cold. "Yes, please," she said.

Muffy Chicago opened a pocket and pulled out a flask. It had her monogram on the outside in curling script: MC. Muffy unscrewed the top and took a sip, then held out the flask toward Megan. "You want some peppermint schnapps?" she said.

Megan didn't really want to drink whatever was in the flask, being all but certain that there were rules against alcohol on campus. She didn't like drunk people, either, having seen more than a few of them make total idiots out of themselves.

"I don't know," said Megan, in a small voice.

"What's the matter?" said Muffy. "Scared?"

•

"So Jonny," said his roommate, Tripper Murphy, "Where are your people from?"

Jonny's eyes flashed angrily for a moment. "I don't know," he said.

"You don't know?" said Tripper. He was blonde and tanned.

"I'm adopted," said Jonny.

"Ah," said Tripper.

"Why, where are your people from?"

"My mother's people are from Newport. Those were the Wickwires. My father's people are from Boston."

It didn't take Jonny long to unpack. He had a few changes of clothing, plus his guitar. He sat down on his bed and began to tune it, although he was no longer able to plug the wires into the amplifier in his neck.

"Frankenstein," said Tripper. "Is that like a Jewish name?"

"I don't know," said Jonny.

"I should think you would know," said Tripper Murphy.

"I told you I was adopted."

"I never knew anybody who was adopted before," said Tripper. He listened to Jonny noodling around on his guitar. "Hey I play guitar too. Let me see yours."

Jonny thought about it. Then he handed his guitar over to Tripper.

The boy started to play. He wasn't bad. He began to sing, in a very loud, operatic voice. "Rock me momma like a wagon wheel! Rock me momma any way you feel! Hey! Hey!"

"Wagon wheel," said Jonny.

"You know this tune?" said Tripper.

"Everybody knows this tune," said Jonny.

"I learned it at sailing camp," said Tripper.

"How come you're called Tripper?" said Jonny.

"It's short for triple. My father is Matthew Murphy the second. My grandfather is Matthew Murphy the first. I'm the third, triple, tripper."

He finished up with "Wagon Wheel."

"Yeah," said Jonny. "Now I'll play you one."

But Tripper didn't give Jonny his guitar back. "Hang on a second," he said. "I want to play another one."

•

"Whaddya like to eat," said Sparkbolt's roommate, Tony Gunkowski, known as Gunk. "You like meat? I like meat." Gunk was huge.

"Meat good," said Sparkbolt.

"Yeah. I like it rare. You like it rare?" said Gunk.

"Rrrr," said Sparkbolt.

"Yeah!" said Gunk. He was putting his socks in his drawer. "What about the ladies? You like the ladies?"

"Rrrr," said Sparkbolt.

"I hear ya!" shouted Gunk. "You and me, we are going to run this school. You doing out for the team?"

"Team," said Sparkbolt.

Gunk, who had a crew cut, nodded. "You must play tackle? You play tackle?"

"Team," said Sparkbolt.

"I thought so," said Gunk. "You're built like a rock, bro."

"Bro!" said Sparkbolt. "Friend!"

"You got it," said Gunk, and held out his fist. Sparkbolt looked at the fist suspiciously, then extended his own fist. Gunk bumped it.

"Meat," said Sparkbolt. "Good."

•

Elaine Bigelow was alphabetizing the books in her bookcase. Merideath lay on her back in her bed, painting her toenails pink. Elaine scrunched up her nose. "Eww," she said, "I hate that smell."

"Sucks to be you," said Merideath.

"Where are your books?" said Elaine. "Didn't you bring any books?"

"They give us the books," said Merideath. "Hel-lo?"

"I mean your own books," said Elaine. She had large brown oval glasses, and a long brown braid of hair that trailed down her back. She was wearing a white blouse that was buttoned all the way up to her neck. Elaine was strangely thin.

"What are you talking about, my own books?" said Merideath.

Elaine looked at her. "You don't——" Then she shut her mouth. Satisfied with the order of her books, she sat back down on her bed with a set of index cards.

"What now?" said Merideath. "You're going to give yourself a quiz?"

"I just wanted to review these elements," she said. "So I remember the atomic weight and the atomic number of the metals."

"So you're doing— voluntary homework?" said Merideath. "Before classes even start?"

"You have to keep ahead," said Elaine.

"You got a boyfriend, Elaine?" said Merideath.

"How could I have a boyfriend?" said Elaine. "I just got here!"

At that moment, Jonny Frankenstein appeared in their doorway. "Hey," he said.

"Jonny," said Merideath, her eyes opening wide. Her lips curled into a smile. "It's so nice to see you."

Jonny shot her a look. "You too, Merry," he said.

"Oh," said Elaine. "Merry! Is that what your friends call you?"

"Who's your roommate?" said Merideath.

"It's me and Tripper Murphy," said Jonny.

"Who's he?" said Merideath.

"Are you kidding?" said Elaine. "They put you in with Tripper Murphy? He's a senior. He's like, the bomb."

"I guess." Jonny didn't sound impressed.

"So what can I do for you Jonny? Do you need— a backrub?"

"Actually, it's your roommate I'm looking for."

"M-me?" said Elaine, blushing.

"Yeah." Jonny looked down, as if embarrassed to be speaking to her. Then he said, "I heard you might have a copy of the chemistry book?"

"Well, yes. Yes I do," said Elaine, getting out and going over to her bookcase. "Here it is. The eighth edition."

"You cannot be serious," said Merideath.

"Are you doing review?" Elaine asked hopefully. "Before classes start?"

"Sort of," said Jonny. "I got an experiment I'm doing."

"Really?" said Elaine. "What kind of experiment?"

Merideath made a face, mocking Elaine.

Jonny looked at Elaine carefully, thoughtfully. "You want me to show you?"

•

Weems sat at his desk, eating out of a very large bag of bar-be-cue potato chips. In the middle of his room, Weems' roommate, Bert Quackenbush, balanced atop of a unicycle. He was listening to headphones and juggling. Weems watched him, horrified and amazed. Every few minutes, Weems would forget that he was eating the chips, and he'd look down at the enormous bag with a sudden shock. Then he'd eat some more chips, turning his cheeks slowly orange.

Bert— who had told Weems to call him Quacky— did a sudden backflip off of the unicycle and landed on his bed. He pulled off his headphones.

"You like marching band music?" said Quacky. "I play the saxophone!"

"I do not like it," said Weems, eating his chips.

"Oh," said Quacky, leaping to his feet. "I forgot I have to finish designing this campaign." He pulled a thick notebook out from underneath his bed. "You like D n D?"

"I do not know what this is," said Weems. "But I suspect I will find this loathsome."

Quacky smiled. "You say that now," he said. "I'm the DM for this campaign we started last spring."

"Dee Emm," said Weems. "These are initials that stand for a thing."

"Dungeonmaster!" said Quacky. "You're saying you never played D and D?" Quacky laughed. "What you been doin' all your life, Weems?"

"Roasting things," said Weems. "Over a little fire."

Quacky looked at Weems curiously. "Hey wait," he said. "What do you have there?" He reached behind Weem's ear, and pulled out a card. "Jack of Diamonds!"

Weems ate another chip. "You are a curious young man."

Quacky looked at Weems curiously. "Maybe that's why they made us roommates!"

"Why would that be?" said Weems.

"We got so much in common!"

"Hmm," said Weems. "Yes, possibly. I suppose—" He paused. The chip he was eating did not crunch beneath this teeth. "Excuse me I—" He raised his hand to his mouth and removed the chip. But it was no chip at all. It was another playing card.

"Jack of Diamonds," said Quacky.

•

Late in the day, after dinner in the cafeteria, which itself had concluded with a speech from the school's headmistress, Mrs. Houndstooth, the students had retired to their rooms. Classes were to begin the next morning at eight.

Destynee and Ankh-hoptet lay on the beds in their room, staring at the ceiling. From other rooms in the old dormitory building, a five story structure covered with ivy, came the sounds of students listening to music, practicing the saxophone, talking softly. Down the hallway, someone was in the girls' bathroom taking a shower.

"I can't believe I'm your roommate," said Destynee, softly.

"It seemed unlikely to me at first," said the Egyptian girl, "that I should have you as my subject. But in time, all shall be ruled by my scepter. By the tomb of seven jackals, you shall be my embalmed slave."

"I was kind of hoping I'd get one of the human girls as a roommate," said Destynee.

"With cinnamon and gold shall we lie in our funerary chamber," said Ankh-hoptet. "We shall like in our sarcophaguses until Amon-Ra wakes us from the nameless sleep."

"Maybe somebody who played soccer," said Destynee.

"Til then, we shall lie in darkness, our bodies wrapped in the gauze soaked in the perfumes of death. All who love us shall know despair, as they behold the wonder of our immortal bosom."

"Would you please shut up?" said Destynee.

"It is not for my slave to order the shutting or closing," warned Ankh-hoptet. "It is only through the immortal life that the opening can become."

"You know, if you talk like that tomorrow, you're going to get us all busted," said Destynee.

"I have warned you!" shouted Ankh-hoptet.

"You're not a mummy any more," said Destynee. "Okay? You're a ninth grader named Annie. You come from Illinois."

"Cairo, Illinois," said Ankh-hoptet.

"Seriously, Ankh-hoptet," said Destynee. "You have to learn how to talk like a normal teenage girl."

There was silence in the room as the mummy considered this. "And how would this enunciation be done?" she said.

Destynee looked over at her roommate. "You want me to give you some pointers?"

"I am ordering you, as my slave, to provide the information that I have requested!"

"Yeah, okay, well, step one, don't be calling me your slave. I'm not your slave. I'm your roommate."

"My roommate. Who shall serve me in my tomb!"

"What's wrong with you?" said Destynee. "Just stop it. You're annoying."

There was silence from the other side of the room. Destynee lay in her bed, listening to the sounds of the dorm. Then she heard another sound— a sniffing, and some hard breathing, coming from her roommate.

"Ankh-hoptet?" said Destynee.

"You're right," said Ankh-hoptet. "I am annoying." She was crying. "I come from a broken home. My Daddy was a mummy."

"It's okay," said Destynee. "You're going to be fine. You just have to stop ordering people around and talking about dead bodies and stuff. It makes people uncomfortable."

"Teach me how to say a thing I should say instead." The mummy snuffed. "I ask you as— my friend. Not as my slave. As my friend."

"Well, what do you want to know how to say?"

"I wish to know— I wish to know how to greet the others!"

"What others?"

"The others in my kingd— ah— this school."

"How do you say hello you mean?"

"Yes," said Ankh-hoptet. "It is this mystery."

"You go, 'Ha-LO-oh.'"

"Ha. Low. Oh."

"No," said Destynee. "You have to emphasize the second syllable. You go, 'Huh-LO-oh."

"Huh LO. Oh?"

"Okay, that's pretty good. And now you have to say a kind of a normal thing, like you say something nice about something somebody is wearing. Instead of ordering them around and stuff."

"You will provide an example!"

"You could go, 'Ha-LO-oh you guuys! I like your UGG Boots!"

There was a moment of thoughtful silence. "What are these boots of Ug? Are they the coffins of the feet of those who trod in dead lands?"

"Well, sort of. They're these boots. I brought a pair, you know those boots I wear? You could say, Hey, I like your UGGS they are so fly!"

"I like, these boots of Ugg," said Ankh-hoptet. "They shall make you fly!"

"Oh-kay," said Destynee. "That's a start I guess."

"Destynee," said Ankh-hoptet. "I ask you this. Do you think— that I shall have friends?"

Destynee rolled over to face the wall. "I don't know," she said. "I hope so. I hope we all have friends." But as she said this, a wave of sadness came upon her, as she remembered her own girlhood, the time before she was diagnosed by the doctors at the Academy for Monsters as a giant enchanted slug. She had wanted so much to be a vampire. Merideath had been her friend, in those early days. But once she'd been diagnosed, Merideath had dropped her like a hot potato. She knew that Merideath was mean spirited, and not a person to look up to. But the memory of being dropped by someone whom she had thought of as her friend still stung.

There was a strange substance on her cheek, and suddenly her heart pounded. She sat up quickly and turned on the light.

"Who is it that disturbs the darkness of my slumbers!" shouted Ankh-hoptet. "I mean— ah— Destynee. Uh. Ha-LO-oh? Why are you so up?"

"I'm okay," she said, wiping her eyes, and as she did so, Destynee realized that she had not cried in a long time. Since morphing into a slug, the salt in her tears had become poisonous to her; it could melt right through her skin.

"You are crying," said the mummy. "Ha-LO-oh. Are you all right?"

"Yes," said Destynee. "It's just I forgot how good it feels. To cry."

•

It was almost midnight now, and Pearl lay in her bed, awake. The dormitory had been quite loud for a while after supper, but one by one, the other students of the Greenblud School had gone to sleep. At eleven o'clock a student proctor named Judy Underhill had knocked on her door and told her it was lights out time. Judy, an athletic looking senior who was, apparently, the head of the field hockey team, had cast an eye upon the empty bed in her room. "No sign of Olga?" she said.

"There is no sign of this one!" said Pearl. "Perhaps she has quavered in fear, at the prospect of what lies before her!"

"Yeah, maybe," said Judy. "Could be her plane got delayed."

"This plane, from where does it come?"

"I don't know," said Judy. "She's foreign."

"We shall welcome her," said Pearl. "Upon her arrival!"

Judy had given Pearl a strange look. "Where are you from, anyway?"

"From Peru!" said Pearl, with great pride. "I am— I am—" She wanted to say, the famous goatsucker of Peru. But they'd been ordered by Vega and the Crow not to give themselves away. It was harder than she had thought. "I am from there!"

"Well," said Judy Underhill. "You take care of yourself. You need anything you let me know. It's a good place, Greenblud, in spite of what you might have heard."

"I have heard only that it is a place where ones scholarship shall be rewarded! And also that—in the past— there have been tragedies."

Judy's eyes grew wide. "You heard about what happened? To James McNinch?"

"Not precisely," said Pearl. "Only that one of the students took his own life. In despair and sadness was this done."

"That's what they told you?" said Judy. She looked down the hallway, as if afraid she might be overheard.

"These are the words that were spoken!"

"It's a lie," said Judy Underhill. "James didn't take his own life."

"No?" said Pearl. "Then how did this loss come about then?"

Judy's voice fell to a whisper. "He—he was murdered."

Pearl sat upright in bed. "No!" she shouted. "It cannot be!"

"Sssh," said Judy, looking down the hall again. "Keep your voice down!"

"But we cannot let this stand unavenged!" shouted Pearl. "Surely, you and I! We shall find the ones with hearts of evil, and introduce them to the sharp steel of revenge!"

"Quiet," said Judy, more forcefully. "What's wrong with you? Don't you know what they'll do if they hear you?"

"I cannot be quiet in the face of injustice!" shouted Pearl. "I shall not rest until—"

Judy Underhill slipped into Pearls room, went over to her bed, and slapped her hand over her mouth. "I said shut up," she said. "I'm the proctor. Okay? When I say, shut up, you shut up? Tell me you understand."

Pearl was still talking beneath Judy's muffling hand. Judy pushed down harder.

"Tell me you understand."

Pearl at last fell silent. She nodded. Judy took her hand away.

"I'll tell you more about it later," she said. "Just go to bed now, okay?" Judy went back to the door, and turned out Pearl's light.

"And for god's sakes, don't say anything, to anyone. They'll come for you."

"Who?" whispered Pearl. "Who is this that will come?"

Judy looked nervously down the hall, and now her face turned even paler. She looked genuinely frightened. "I have to go," she said, and then closed the door.

Pearl lay there in the dark, thinking about what she had heard. It was going to be very hard for her to pretend to be human, harder than she had thought. It wasn't living a life without a stinger, or without wings, that was going to be the challenge. The challenge was going to be remaining silent, when she encountered a situation that cried out for justice.

She did not know how humans did it.

Pearl must have dozed off eventually, because the next thing she knew, her door was creaking open again. Pearl looked at her alarm clock. It read 3:30 AM.

The lights in the hallway were dim, but she could see the silhouette of a large, lumpy figure standing there in the door.

"Judy?" said Pearl uncertainly, but even as she did, she knew that this was someone else entirely. Pearl felt her heartbeat quicken, and remembered what her proctor had said. They'll come for you.

"Is not Judy," said the voice, and the stranger stepped forward into the room.

"You shall speak your name!" said Pearl. "You shall not hunker in the dark, like a creature of the night!"

The stranger flicked on the light switch, and there she was: a large, round girl with black hair tied back in a tight bun. Her eyebrows were extraordinarily thick and hairy, like a pair of wooly-bear caterpillar. In her right hand she carried a heavy suitcase. In her right hand was a bag of something Pearl recognized instantly.

It was fencing equipment—a pair of swords and a mask.

"Is Olga," she said.

5.

Good Night Nobody

Looking back on it later, Falcon would think the first day at Greenblud in the same way you might remember a day spent in a foreign capital whose language you did not speak. From the moment his alarm clock went off, he found himself fumbling to understand the customs of what felt like a very alien civilization indeed, except that the creatures whose habits he did not quite understand were human beings. He could not quite believe, as he came out of the shower in the boy's bathroom, wearing a white robe, that the other boys could not look at him and detect his distance and difference. Of course, it had only been two years since Falcon had departed Cold River, Maine for the Academy for Monsters in the Bermuda Triangle— two years since he himself had gone to middle school with other people he thought were human.

But the two years among monsters had changed him; he had learned the differences between zombies and vampires, were-bears and Frankensteins, Sasquatches and Chupakabras and mummies. Each monster had its own distinct culture and history. There were times when Falcon though that there were some things he'd never get straight, like the differences between fauns and Squonks.

But human beings, especially teenaged ones, were harder to understand than Squonks. And his job was made even more difficult by the fact that he was disguised as one of them. So he couldn't stop to ask questions, like, why are you wearing sunglasses indoors? Or why do you wear your hair in front of your eyes so you can't see? Or, why do you have a giant hole pierced in your ear? He felt the strangers' eyes upon him at breakfast in the school cafeteria that morning, and he felt them in the hall way as he made his way to his first class. It seemed like all the ninth graders did at Greenblud was check each other out, and find some flaw.

Falcon's new roommate, Malcolm, wasn't much help, not least because he seemed every bit as lost as Falcon. "I come from Montana," he explained. "From a town called Glump Corners." When Falcon looked at him as if expecting more of an explanation, Malcolm just said, "It's a farm town."

The students at Greenblud were sent to the Academy from towns across the nation, as well as more than a few countries overseas. They were tall and short, dark and pale, fat and thin. But neither Falcon nor Malcolm seemed to be able to understand any of them. It seemed, even on this first day, as if everyone already understood some secret that had not been explained.

Falcon got to his first class, English Literature, at 8 AM. Many of Falcon's friends-in-disguise were in the class as well, including Max and Megan and Pearl. Ankh-hopet sat in the front row next to

Sparkbolt. The class was full of people talking and laughing.

There was a girl sitting next to Falcon who was wearing lots of makeup. Her hair was piled on top of her head. "I hate literature," she said to Falcon.

"I don't hate it," said Falcon. "But I'm no good at it."

"I hate everything I'm no good at," she said. "But I'm good at a lot of things." She raised an eyebrow. "What about you? Are you good at things?"

Falcon wasn't sure what to tell her. "I'm Muffy Chicago," she said.

"Falcon," he said.

"You got a roommate?" she asked. "Or a single?"

"I'm roommates with this guy Malcolm," Falcon said. "He's from Montana."

"Eew, gross," said Muffy. "I got this girl from Maine, Megan." Muffy nodded at Megan, who was sitting across the room by herself. "She's so boring."

Falcon was about to say, She's my friend, but then he remembered that they weren't supposed to know each other. So instead, Falcon just said, "That's too bad."

"Let's kill our roommates," said Muffy. "You want?"

"Would we have to actually kill them?" said Falcon. "Maybe we could just poison them a little."

Muffy laughed. "You're cute," she said.

The door swung open and in walked a teacher, a breathless young man in a tweed coat with horn rim glasses and a mop of brown hair. He wrote his name on the board. MR. CONNELLY. "Well, well, well," he said. "What do we have here. A room full of freshman. Splendid. This is a class in English. But specifically it's a class in writing. This fall I'm going to have you read stories. And then I'll have you write some stories of your own. By the end of the semester you'll have a better understanding of the workings of short stories, as well as a better understanding of yourselves. Sound good? Great. Okay, you, what's your name?"

He pointed at a large boy in the front row. "Gunk," he said.

"Ah, Mister Gunk. Lovely. Now what's your favorite story?"

"Uh," said Gunk.

"Anything you've read recently? Or something you remember from childhood?"

"Uh," said Gunk.

"Hm," said Mr. Connelly. "We're not getting anywhere. What about you, next to Mr. Gunk?"

"Sparkbolt."

"Yes. What's your favorite story?"

"Road Not Taken," said Sparkbolt. "Good."

"Ah, yes, that's a delightful poem, but what about a story? Anything in prose?"

"I read around in Faulkner this summer," said Tripper Murphy.

"Around you say?" said Mr. Connelly. "What specifically?"

"As I Lay Dying," said Tripper. "The Sound and the Fury."

Mr. Connelly nodded, impressed. "Those are challenging books," he said.

"I like a challenge," said Tripper.

"Rrr," said Sparkbolt.

"Yes, Mr. Sparkbolt?" said Mr. Connelly. "What did you read?"

"Moon," said Sparkbolt.

"Moon?"

"Goodnight Moon," said Sparkbolt.

"Ah, yes, indeed. Good night moon! By Margaret Wise Brown. A classic!" Mr. Connelly was pacing around the room now. He whisked his glasses off and waved them through the air. "Who wouldn't want to live in that great green room? A world of such peace!"

There was quiet for a moment as everyone thought about it.

"Good night, nobody," said Sparkbolt. His voice quavered.

"I know," said Mr. Connelly. "That's always seemed to me like the saddest page in all of literature. Goodnight, nobody! I remember when I was a child, how that page sometimes used to make me cry."

Muffy rolled her eyes and looked at Falcon. "Oh, My, God," she mouthed at him.

"Are there any other books you remember from childhood that made you cry? Anyone?"

There was an embarrassed silence in the class. Then Malcolm spoke up. "Charlottes Web totally made me cry," he said. "At the end, when the spider dies, I thought I'd just sob my eyes out."

Milton put his hands over his ears and shouted, "No spoilers!"

Muffy wrote a note on a piece of paper and handed it to Falcon. It said, He's so gay. She nodded toward Malcolm.

Falcon wasn't certain how to respond. He nodded noncommitally.

"Seriously," said Malcolm. "I didn't leave my bed for days after I read that book." People laughed a little bit. "Finally I just wrapped my self up in a blanket and sat by the fire and started Stuart Little. Which is almost as sad!"

Sparkbolt sighed sadly. "Fire bad," he said.

•

When the bell rang, and the students scrambled to their feet to get to the next class, Muffy leaned over to Falcon and asked his name. When Falcon told her, something in her eyes twinkled. "My roommate, Idiot Megan, says she knows you."

"Yeah," said Falcon. "We, uh, met on the bus from the airport."

"You want to come to our room tonight?" said Muffy. "Maybe we can gross her out if we try."

"Uh, okay," said Falcon. "That's sounds all right. Should I like, ask my roommate to come, too?"

"Who's your roommate?"

"Him," Falcon said nodding toward Malcolm, who was up at the front of the room having a conversation with Mr. Connelly.

Muffy rolled her eyes, as if Falcon's question was a joke. "I don't think so," she said.

•

After classes that first day, Bert Quackenbush asked Weems if he wanted to go to a special meeting.

"Meeting,what is the meeting?" asked Weems.

"Robotics club," said Quacky.

"It is building a robot?" said Weems.

"We're all building robots," said Quacky. "Not big ones. But big enough to do stuff. I want to make one that can operate a Three-D Printer. And use the Three-D printer to make a copy of itself."

"How clever this is," said Weems.

Quacky grinned. "There will be snacks," he said.

"Snacks," said Weems. "Are they crunchy?"

"We got barbecue potato chips," said Quacky. "And Cheese Dinkles."

"It has the Dinkles," said Weems. "Yes. Perhaps we might build a robot with you. Perhaps one that could print some flowers. For the Beloved!"

"You're funny," said Quacky.

"It has no idea," said Weems.

•

At football practice that afternoon, the coach, Mr. Wilson, paced up and down the sidelines with a clipboard and a whistle. "All right boys," he said. "It's time to see what you're made of."

"Rrr," said Sparkbolt.

"Let's go," said Gunk. The boys lined up in formation, with Gunk in the quarterback position and Sparkbolt playing end. Gunk counted off the play, and then stepped backward to prepare for the pass. But the boys playing against him broke through the defenses easily, and in a moment, Gunk was sacked. Mr. Wilson blew his whistle.

"Okay, okay," he said. "Let's switch positions. You, Sparkbolt. This time you play right tackle. I want you to create a wall around Gunk here."

"Wall," said Sparkbolt.

"Attaboy."

Gunk counted off the play and the ball was hiked to him. Again the other players swarmed toward him, but this time they found it hard to get around Sparkbolt, who blocked Gunk completely, and growled menacingly as he did so. Gunk, searching to find someone to pass to, finally tossed the ball to Sparkbolt. For a moment Sparkbolt stood there looking at the ball in his hands, wondering what to do next. Then he growled again and began to run. One after another, opposing players attempted to bring him down, but Sparkbolt just kept running. At last he was in the clear, and

Sparkbolt crossed over the goal line with the football tucked neatly beneath his arm.

"Rrrr!" shouted Sparkbolt, and spiked the ball on the ground.

"Whoa," said Gunk.

"Man can play," said Mr. Wilson.

"That's not a man, that's a mountain," said a boy named Lemon, who was playing center.

"The Mountain!" said Gunk. "That's what we should call you, Sparkbolt! Hey! That's my roommate! The Mountain."

Sparkbolt rejoined the rest of the team to cheers and applause. He smiled self consciously. "Friends," he said. "Good."

•

At dinner, Desynee and Ankh-hoptet were sitting at a table with Elaine Bigelow, eating tacos, when Pearl came by with her roommate, Olga. "My friends!" she said. "We shall join you!"

Destynee and Pearl and Elaine Bigelow looked up at them.

"Is good?" said Olga. She was absolutely enormous and just the sight of her holding her tray was astonishing.

"Sure," said Destynee. "We were just talking."

"This is my roommate!" announced Pearl. "Olga Vzlynrßk, from the village of Bharf! Across the snows of the north she has travelled, to be with us here!"

"Is good," said Olga.

"Oh, it must be so cold there," said Elaine.

"And yet her spirit is warm!" said Pearl. "To New Hampshire she has come, to bring her considerable strength and daring! We are pledged, she and I! To be friends!"

Elaine looked at Pearl with confusion. "Where are you from, Pearl?"

"I come from Trujillo, in Peru! Between the mountains and the sea! I am—la—, la— uh— la—-!"

"Is singing now?" said Olga.

"La—longing for my home," said Pearl, sweating. "It is a journey of thousands of miles, to the land of my birth!"

"I'd love to go to Peru some day," said Elaine. "There is so much to learn about the Incas."

"And so we shall travel there— you and I!" said Pearl. "We shall embark upon this quest!"

Olga nodded. "Is good," she said.

"Hey," said Elaine. "Did you hear there's going to be an election?"

"Really?" said Destynee. "For what?"

"Class officers," said Elaine. "President and vice-president. Secretary, Treasurer."

"Does what?" said Olga.

"The president?" said Elaine. "The president of the class runs things, you know, plans events, represents us with the administration."

Ankh-hoptet put down her taco. "The ruler," she said somberly. "It is this one whose destiny it is to reign, in darkness and in terror."

Elaine wrinkled her nose. "Well, not exactly," she said.

"Now it begins," said Ankh-hoptet. "The dawning of my dynasty. I shall rule this class, and in embalmed darkness bring forth the underworld."

"Yeah, okay," said Elaine. "But you should make sure we have an awesome prom, too."

Ankh-hoptet looked around the cafeteria somberly. "My subjects shall fear my royal powers."

"Hey," said Destynee. "You have to get elected first."

"Elected?" said Ankh-hoptet. "Who would challenge my right to rule?"

"Well, I heard that one guy is running. You know, the hunk with the intense eyes, lives in a single?"

"Jonny Frankenstein?" said Destynee.

"No, his roommate. The hunkamunka. Tripper Murphy."

Ankh-hoptet's eyes turned dark. "He shall not impede my kingdom."

"I don't know," said Elaine. "He's pretty hot."

Olga nodded. "Is hot," she said.

•

Falcon knocked on Megan and Muffy's door.

"Go away," said a voice from inside, and Falcon could tell that Megan was upset. He swung open the door.

"Megan, it's okay," he said. But as he stepped into the room, he saw that Muffy Chicago was alone. She was sitting on the edge of her bed holding her face in her hands. "Oh, I'm sorry—" he said, embarassed.

"Oh," said Muffy. "It's you."

"I thought you were Megan," he said.

"I wish I was Megan," Muffy muttered.

"What's wrong?" said Falcon. "Why are you crying?"

"Like it's any of your business," said Muffy.

"Falcon," said Megan, coming into the room from the hallway.

"How do you two know each other again?" asked Muffy.

"Oh, we don't," said Falcon swiftly. "I mean, not really. We rode the bus from the airport together."

"You're roommates with that guy," said Muffy. She wiped the tears from her face.

"What guy?" said Megan. She went into the room and sat down upon her bed.

"You know, that Malcolm. The one with the earring? He's so gay."

"You shouldn't—" said Megan. "You shouldn't use that word like that."

"What, gay?" said Muffy. "But he is. Isn't he?" She looked at Falcon.

"I don't know," said Falcon. "I never thought about it."

"Well, think about it," said Muffy. "Middle of the night, you could find somebody creeping up next to you."

"That's a mean thing to say," said Falcon.

"Whatever," said Muffy. She reached under her pillow and pulled out a small silver flask. "You like to party, Falcon?"

"What?" said Falcon. "What is that?"

"It's peppermint schnapps," said Muffy. "Have a shot!"

"No way," said Falcon. "I'm not drinking that." He looked at Megan. "Are you drinking that? You know that can expel you for that."

"Who's going to know?" said Muffy.

"Seriously, Megan," said Falcon. "You're drinking alcohol?"

Megan shrugged. "I don't know," she said.

"Megan—" said Falcon.

"Hey," said Muffy. "No one's making you stay. Why don't you head back to your boyfriend?"

"He's not my boyfriend," said Falcon. "What kind of thing is that to—?"

"Prove it," said Muffy, holding the flask toward him.

Megan looked at Falcon, and his heart broke for her. She'd never really recovered from the time she'd spent as a prisoner in the Entangling Sails of the windmill on the island of the Guardians. She'd found out that her sisters were not dead, and there'd been a great reunion of the three Crofton girls, but now here she was, thousands of miles from home, alone again, stuck in a double with Muffy Chicago.

"Please, Falcon," said Megan, looking at him beseechingly. "Just so you know what it's like."

Falcon stood by Muffy and Megan's bed, looking at the flask, wondering what choice he should make now.

6.

The Perils of Bouncing

The next day, Max stood in a courtyard, playing hackey-sack with some of his new friends, a long haired guy named Cheese and a roly-poly guy called Pigpen. Johnny Frankenstein sat near them on a wall, playing his guitar.

"Ooh, good one, man," said Cheese. He wore a white t-shirt with a red star in the middle of the chest. He ran back, spun, and fielded the hackey-sack with the side of his foot, then kicked it high into the air.

"I got it, I got it," said Max, trying to get under it.

"Out of control," said Pigpen.

Max headed the hackey-sack, which rebounded toward the ground. Max kicked it high again toward Cheese.

"Hey look," said a voice. "The retard squad." Max turned to see Gunk standing there, wearing an athletic shirt with a big number on the back. Sparkbolt stood next to him.

"Yo," said Max. "That's not cool."

"Yo," said Gunk. "Why don't you play a real game?"

"A real game?" said Cheese. "Like what, Gunk, football?"

"Duh," said Gunk.

"Duh," said Sparkbolt.

"Hey man," said Max. "Everybody gets to play their own game."

"Ya think?" said Gunk. He stepped forward and grabbed the hackey-sack away from Cheese.

"Give that back," said Cheese.

"Hey Sparkbolt, go long," said Gunk. Sparkbolt ran, and Gunk passed the hackey sack to him. Then Sparkbolt threw it back. The two of them passed it back and forth, with Cheese in the middle, reaching up and trying—and failing—to get it back.

"Out of control," said Pigpen.

"Hey man," said Max to Gunk. "What's wrong with you? Give it back to him."

"Make me," said Gunk.

"You want me to hit you?" said Max. "Seriously? Who does that?"

"Chicken," said Gunk.

"I'm not chicken, I just don't hit people," said Max. "Even if they are lardbrains."

"Who are you calling lardbrain," said Cheese.

"Hey Sparkbolt, is this guy a friend of yours, seriously?" said Max.

"Friend!" said Sparkbolt. "Good!"

Gunk reached forward and with one hand picked up Cheese by the collar. The boy sputtered and squiggled a few feet off the ground.

"Out of control?" said Pigpen.

But at that moment Gunk suddenly let Cheese go. Sparkbolt pulled him by the shoulder, spun him around and punched him in the jaw. Gunk said, "Oof," and fell to the ground.

"Bad," said Sparkbolt. "RRarr!".

"Dude," said Gunk, "What the hell!"

Mr. Connelly came rushing over. "What's going on here?" he said.

"Nothing," said Gunk.

"Let's break it up," said Mr. Connelly. "Come on, let's go."

"Rrar," said Sparkbolt.

"You just made a big mistake, Sparky," said Gunk.

"You make mistake," said Sparkbolt.

"I said break it up," said Mr. Connelly.

Gunk got up off the ground and dusted himself off, then slunk away.

"Out of control!" said Pigpen.

Sparkbolt stood growlingly mournfully for a moment as Gunk walked off. Then he reached down and picked up the hackey-sack, and put it back in Cheese's hand. Tears shimmered in his eyes.

"Friend bad," he said.

•

Falcon lay on his back in his dorm room bed, reading a book called The Life of Organisms, his textbook for intro bio. In one hand he held a yellow highlighter, which he used to emphasize parts of the the text that seemed like they might well wind up on the quiz. He read the first paragraph of the chapter, and then highlighted the first sentence. Then he highlighted the last sentence. He thought about what he had read for a moment, then highlighted the two sentences in the middle. Now the whole first paragraph was yellow. He closed the book for a moment, trying to remember what it was he had just read. Nothing came to mind.

Malcolm, Falcon's roommate, stood before the mirror above the built-in bureau that the boys shared, tying a tie and watching his own reflection. "Did you read this Bio?" Falcon asked.

"Sure I read it," said Malcolm. "It's about osmosis. I thought it was pretty cool."

"Cool,' said Falcon. "Yeah, that's not the first word that comes to mind."

"But it is," said Malcolm. Now he was brushing his hair. "Osmosis means the way molecules of a solvent move through a semipermeable membrane from a less concentrated solution into a more concentrated one. If you wait long enough the concentrations on each side of the membrane are the same." He turned to look at Falcon. "Right?"

"Yeah," said Falcon. "I guess."

"It's also a pretty good way of thinking about the way people learn things," said Malcolm. "Like, sometimes you learn through reading, or through a lecture or something. But other times, you just learn things because the knowledge passes through you. Like a solution through a membrane. You look up and you realize you learned something without even knowing it."

"And that's—" Falcon said. "A good thing?"

"Sometimes," said Malcolm. "Like the way you learn a song, maybe. You hear it, and the next thing you know, you can sing it. But it can be not so good too, I guess. Like, people come to believe something because they get surrounded by other people who believe that same thing. Whether it's true or not. Like, I don't know. People who think Elvis is alive."

"Wait," said Falcon. "Elvis isn't alive?"

"Ha ha, very funny," said Malcom. "So tell me how I look. Good, right?"

"I guess," said Falcon. "Why?"

"I'm trying out for the a capella group, the Bludstones?" said Malcolm. "I'm so psyched."

"An a capella group?" said Falcon. "What's that?"

"Seriously?" said Falcon. "Like on Glee. It's a singing group. How can you not know that, have you been on Mars or something?"

Falcon wanted to explain, no, actually he'd been on Monster Island for two years. But he couldn't go there. Instead, Falcon asked Malcolm something else.

"Hey, can I ask you something? Do people ever make fun of you because of your eyes?"

"Eyes?" said Malcolm. "What about them?"

"You know," said Falcon. "You've got one black eye and one green eye."

Malcolm turned around and looked in the mirror. He screamed. "OH MY GOD YOU'RE RIGHT! Falcon! MY EYES ARE DIFFERENT COLORS!"

Falcon felt uncertain for a moment. His roommate did know about his eyes before this, right? Then Malcolm turned around and smiled. "Had you," he said.

"No you didn't," said Falcon.

"So yeah. I used to worry about it. That it made me different. But then I realized that the thing that made me different was my secret weapon. That it was the thing that made me special. One of the things that made me special, anyhow." He winked at Falcon. "What about you? Anyone ever give you a hard time about your eyes being different colors?"

"Wait, my eyes are different colors?" said Falcon.

"Yeah, nice try," said Malcolm. "Seriously, it's a little weird that we both have wacky eyes and we're roommates. You think they planed it that way?"

"I hope not," said Falcon.

"You have to admit, it makes us a-may-zing," said Malcolm.

"Yeah, okay," said Falcon. "We're amazing."

"All right," said Malcolm. "I gotta go. I'll see you after the tryouts."

"Where are these tryouts," said Falcon.

"Across campus," said Malcolm. "In the gym."

"Yeah?" said Falcon. "Okay." He looked out the window of the dorm. It was dark out. Falcon thought it was remarkable, how much earlier it got dark here in northern New England than in the Bermuda Triangle. Back on Monster Island, the sun would still have been shining down on the palm trees.

"What?" said Malcolm.

"Just— be careful," said Falcon.

"Of course," said Malcolm. "I'm always careful." He bowed. "And now, to you, Falcon Quinn, O Roommate of the Many-Colored Eyes, I bid you, adieu!"

Malcolm left the room with a great flourish. Falcon heard his footsteps going down the hallway, and then the door at the hall's end opened and closed with a heavy clang. For a moment, Falcon lay in his bed, thinking about his roommate. He wondered what it was like for him, growing up in Montana. Was it lonely, being Malcolm in the place he had grown up? Then Falcon remembered his own childhood, the long days he'd spent in the cabin with his grandmother, Gamm, by the shores of Cold Pond in Maine. He'd thought he was an orphan, back then, that his parents were both dead.

Well, maybe that wasn't so far from the truth, Falcon thought. Even though, as he'd learned, his parents were alive, there had been

plenty of times in the last two years when they may as well have
been. He wondered what it was he had done to make them love each
other more than they loved him.

Falcon picked up his biology book and began the chapter on
osmosis again. He highlighted a few more paragraphs, then paused
when he realized that once again, he'd highlighted every word on the
page. And he still couldn't remember what he'd read.

His black eye burned softly in its socket.

"Arrgh," Falcon said, and threw the highlighter on the floor.
You see, he thought to himself. Even though you've been through
the Bland-a-tron, you're still the thing you've always been— the
two-hearted angel. The good side of him wanted to forgive his
parents, to be compassionate and loving and move on. The other
side of him, the one he felt burning in his black eye, wanted to find
the Crow and Vega and blast them with one of his fireballs.

Falcon got up and went to the window. A cool autumn breeze
blew gently through the screen. From his room, Falcon could see the
long quad of Greenblud Academy, dark at this hour. A couple was
walking across the lawn, a young man and a woman, holding hands.
The woman was pushing a stroller. The sound of a baby crying
reached Falcon's ears, and he watched as the woman reached into
the stroller and raised a baby to her shoulder. He could hear her
cooing gently to the child. "You're okay," she said. "You're going
to be all right."

The father stepped into the light, and Falcon saw, with a shock that it was his English teacher, Mr. Connelly. But his face looked entirely different than the one Falcon had seen in class. Even from this distance, Falcon could see this was the face of a man in love. He stood in front of his wife and encircled her, and their child, in his arms.

Part of Falcon was gently moved by this tender display, thought that it was wonderful that Mr. Connelly had this love in his life.

And another part wanted to find Mr. Connelly and blast him with a fireball, from his black, dark eye. If I can't be loved, Falcon thought. No one can.

Recognizing that he'd begun to think thoughts that were more than a little dangerous, given the mission that he and the other monsters-in-disguise had undertaken, Falcon turned from the window with a sudden desire to snap himself out of his mood. I should take a walk or something, he thought.

Grabbing his room key, Falcon headed out the door and down the hall.

I should go and see Megan, he thought. They'd almost been boyfriend and girlfriend two years ago, in the days after they'd first arrived at the Academy for Monsters. One night, after Quimby—the floating head—had gotten loose, they'd chased after him through Grisleigh Hall, trying to get Quimby back into his jar. While they'd let Quimby escape through their fingers, he and Megan had still had a moment where they stood by the clock up in the tower, and they had almost kissed. Falcon had thought that he was on the verge of going out with Megan for a while, and then she'd disappeared, winding up as the hostage of the Guardians. They'd kept her trapped in the sails of a a windmill on Guardian Island for a long time, until Falcon had helped to free her. But Megan was never really herself after that, even though she'd been reunited with her sisters, whom she'd mourned for years. It made Falcon think that there were some bad things that happened to people that you could never get over. No matter what happened to you later on in your life, you always carried the trouble of your past with you.

That was why she was drinking that awful stuff that Muffy Chicago was giving to her. It wasn't because she wanted to impress Muffy; Falcon could tell that Megan didn't really like her. But there was something in Megan that still ached, from all the things she'd been through. He'd stood there in their room the other night, as Megan handed him the flask. For a moment he'd been tempted to take it, in order to keep from throwing up another wall between himself and Megan. But then his black eye had started to burn, and he just handed the flask back to her. What's wrong with you, he'd said to her. You know this is stupid. Don't you?

I don't know what I know, Megan said.

I know something, said Muffy. I know you should leave.

He'd stormed out, heading all the way back to his room, feeling his anger smoulder. He got back to the room, found the light off, and he just lay down in his bed with all his clothes on. Malcolm had whispered at him through the dark. "Hey Falcon— you okay?"

But Falcon hadn't replied.

So it was to Megan's room that Falcon headed now, not only because he knew he'd said the wrong thing to her the day before, but also because he needed a friend of his own at this hour. And there was no one who knew him as well as Megan, not even Max. His Sasquatch friend was a force for good, a big, joyful presence. But things just bounced off of Max; nothing could affect his generous, abundant personality. Max was a good friend to have; being around him was like warming yourself by a fire. But if your heart felt heavy, Megan was the one to turn to.

He knew what he wanted to tell her, too. Listen, I'm sorry I yelled at you about the flask. I know why you want to drink that stuff. There are times I think about that too.

Megan lived in the next dorm over, an ivy covered building called MOSSBACK. He climbed the heavy iron stairs that led up to the second floor. He heard his footsteps echoing as he climbed.

Falcon checked his watch as he walked down the hall. It was just shy of eight o'clock. Visiting hours lasted until nine.

"Megan?" he said, knocking on her door. There was no answer. "Hello?" He tried the handle, and the door swung open. A single desk light on Megan's side of the room was on. "Megan? You there?"

He knew it was wrong to enter her room without permission, but something in his hearts urged him forward.

And there was Megan, lying on the bed. The flask was on the desk next to her. "Hey," he said. "Are you okay?"

For a moment he was afraid that Megan was drunk, or sick, or—who knows?— dead. But she opened her eyes, and looked at him. "Oh, Falcon," she said, and her voice quavered. "I'm so sorry."

"Hey," he said. "It's okay. What's going on?"

"Oh, I had a big fight with Muffy. She was carrying on like she does, you know. Said a bunch of mean things about people. About your roommate. About you."

"What did she say?"

Megan shuddered. "What do you think?" she said. She nodded toward the flask. "Then she tried to get me to drink that stuff again, and I said no. I was thinking about what you said. You were right, it is stupid."

"I shouldn't have said that."

"Yes, you should," said Megan. "I'm just— I don't know, I'm messed up."

Falcon reached up and touched the side of her face. "It's okay," said Falcon. "Being messed up is normal."

Megan laughed, and as she did it occurred to Falcon that he hadn't heard her laugh since they left Monster Island. "Hey," he said. "Hey Megan."

She looked at his lips, and then she looked at his eyes. Her mouth was slightly open. Their faces drew closer together. Falcon could count the freckles on Megan's nose.

"Hey!" shouted a voice. "Dudes! What's happening!"

Falcon turned. There was Max, the size of a bus, standing in the door. "Whoa. Am I like, interrupting something?"

"No," said Falcon and Megan simultaneously.

"I was just wondering what was going on," said Max. "I just got back from auditioning— for that singing group? You think I'll make it?" He threw back his head and bellowed. "Swing low! Sweet Chaaaariot! Coming for to carry me hoooo—-"

"I bet you got a good shot at it, Max," said Falcon.

"So what do you want to do now. Maybe go out and bounce around before lights out?"

"Bounce?" said Megan. "What do you mean, bounce?."

"You know," said Max. "Bouncing."

"I don't know how to bounce."

"Sure you do! Everybody's good at bouncing! I mean, all you gotta do is bounce."

Falcon sighed inwardly. As along as Max was his friend, he would never have a quiet moment. "Okay, fine," said Falcon.

"Okay fine, what?" said Max.

"Okay, let's go bouncing," said Falcon.

"Awesome," said Max. "Let's do it!" Megan sighed, then got up out of her bed. They left her room and walked down the hall. "I don't even know what we're doing," said Megan.

They descended the stairs, and came out on the dark quad. "Okay, man," said Max. "Here we are! Let's bounce!"

"Max, you have to—"

"Here, I'll go first," said Max, and he ran down the sidewalk, and leaped into the air, landed on his feet and then leaped again. Then he raised his hands into the air and shouted. "I'M ALIVE!! I'M HAPPY!! WE'RE BOUNCING!"

Then he walked back to where his friends were standing. "Whoa, I feel so much better," he said. "Cleans out the whole system!" He nodded toward Falcon. "Okay, man, your turn."

"Max, this is stupid—" said Falcon.

"Yeah, kind of," said Max.

"Max, I don't think I want to—"

"I'll do it," said Megan, and started running down the sidewalk. She jumped into the air and shouted. "I'm all right!" she shouted. "I'm okay!" She landed, then jumped again. "I'M BOUNCING!" Megan turned back to Falcon, then smiled ear to ear. "He's right. It does clean out the system."

"What system is this?" said Falcon.

"The system of stupid," said Max.

"Come on, Falcon, have a bounce," said Megan. "You know you want to."

Falcon was pretty sure he did not want to, but there wasn't much choice now. "Okay," he said. "Fine." He ran down the sidewalk and leaped into the air. "I'M ALIVE!" he shouted. "I'M ALIVE!" He landed on his feet and turned back to look at his friends. And there they were—Megan Crofton and Max Parsons— his friends from childhood. He remembered standing at the bus stop two years ago when Bus 13 had picked them up and taken them off to Academy for Monsters.   His hearts filled with love for them both.

Falcon ran back toward Max and Megan, and put his arms around them and squeezed.   And without giving it much thought, he then reached forward and kissed Megan right on the lips.   Max took a big step back from his friends.   He said, "Dude."

Megan kissed him back.   For a long moment they stood there together, their lips softly brushing against each others'.   Falcon smelled the smell of her shampoo, and felt the exhalation of breath against his neck.

There was a strong, warm wind, and now Falcon felt her hair against his cheek. A warm light began to surround them both as well.

"Uh-oh," said Max.

"What?" said Falcon.   "What's uh-oh?"

"Falcon," said Megan, looking at the top of his head.   "You're glowing."

In other circumstances, Falcon might have had to ask her what she was talking about.   But Falcon knew exactly what she meant by this.   His halo had begun to glow again.   His wings were straining against the inside of his shirt.   He knew that this was happening because something similar was happening to Megan, the wind elemental.   A strong breeze was starting to blow from her.   Leaves by the side of the sidewalk were lifted in a sudden whorl.

"You guys gotta calm down," said Max.   "Remember Mrs. R said you could revert, like, if you—"

"Aaaggghh," said Falcon, and the back of his shirt suddenly ripped off, and his angel wings spread out behind him. His halo glowed brightly over his head. Megan reached forward and took his hand. Her hair blew around her face in the fury of her wind-forces.

"Seriously, go back to being humans, man," said Max. "Somebody could come along here any second, and we'll be busted!"

"Falcon—" said Megan. She was starting to grow translucent. "I'm starting to—" She flickered out completely for a moment, then reappeared as a whirling, swirling half-shadow. "Falcon—!" she said, more alarmed. Her wind elemental nature was completely taking over now. "Help me!"

"This is bad," said Max. "This is really bad."

From the far side of the quad, they heard voices. People were shouting and laughing. They were coming this way.

"Okay," said Max. "Look. You guys monstered up because you were happy. Now you gotta think of something sad."

"Something sad?" said Megan. "But I can't think of anything s—" And then she vanished.

Wind rushed around Falcon and Max, their hair blowing in their faces. Then it was gone.

"We took care of him!" said one of the approaching voices.

"Yeah, we fixed his wagon," said another.

"Honestly, I don't know why they let people like that in here," said a third, whom Falcon immediately recognized as Muffy Chicago.

Falcon looked at Max. "Where's Megan?" he said.

Max shrugged. "I don't know man, but you gotta put the wings and halo away now."

There was more laughing from across the quad.

"Megan?" said Falcon, into the empty air. "Come back!"

"Dude," said Max. "They're coming."

"She's gone, Max," said Falcon. "She's gone."

As he said the word gone, the halo over Falcon's head disappeared, and his wings fluttered and withdrew back into his shoulder blades. A feather drifted onto the ground.

"Dude," said Max. "Put your shirt back on, okay?"

"Hey," said one of the voices. "What was that light?"

"Hide," said Max. "We gotta hide!" Falcon picked his torn shirt off the ground, and the two of them ran behind the corner of Mossback Hall.

"Who's there?" shouted Tripper. As the group drew near, Falcon recognized the other two voices as well— it was Gunk and and Muffy Chicago.

"Nobody," said Max. Falcon pulled his shirt back on.

The three students turned the corner, laying eyes upon them.

"Well, well. If it isn't the new kids on the block," said Muffy.

"What are you doing out?" said Gunk. "It's study hour."

"Yeah, man, but it's an awesome night!" said Max. "Look at the stars!"

"The stars," said Tripper, contemptuously.

"What are you doing out," said Falcon.

"Hey, it's none of your business," said Muffy. "We'll do what we feel like."

"Well, I guess we can do that too," said Falcon.

Gunk laughed. "He says he guesses he can do that too."

"What's your name," said Tripper.

"I'm Falcon Quinn. This is Max."

"Falcon Quinn?" said Tripper, smiling. "That's really your name?"

"Do we have a problem?" said Falcon. "Because if we have a problem, can we just cut to the chase?"

"Man says he wants to cut to the chase," said Tripper. He looked at Gunk. "Guess we oughta give him what he asks for."

Gunk stepped forward, and with a sudden move, pinned Falcon up against the wall with one hand. "What do you think, Falcon Quinn?" he said. "Are you seeing stars now?"

Falcon felt his black eye heating up. He knew that he should hold in his anger, that if he didn't he might well revert to his monster form again. But it was getting harder and harder to resist.

At that moment, though, Gunk himself was raised into the air. His arms and legs flailed around. Max had grabbed the young man

by the neck and was holding him aloft with one hand. Max threw
his head back and roared, Sasquatch-style.

"Yo!" said Tripper. "Put him down! What's the matter with
you!"

But Max's dander was up. He just turned his head and put his
face into Tripper Murphy's and then he roared again. Then he
dropped Gunk onto the ground.

"What the heck was that?" said Tripper.

"He hurt my neck," said Gunk.

"You don't mess with my friends," said Max. "Okay? It's not
nice."

Tripper kicked Gunk in the shins. "Get up," he said. "Come on.
Let's go. They're so queer."

"Hey, you should be nice to people!" Max shouted.

"You think this is over?" said Tripper. "You're wrong. This is
how it starts!"

Tripper, Gunk, and Muffy walked back toward the dorms.
"Yeah," said Muffy. "Talk to your boyfriend Malcolm. Ask him
how he likes the stars." The three of them laughed.

Their voices faded as they walked away. But the last thing
Falcon saw was Tripper Murphy casting a glance over one shoulder
in their direction. He didn't look at Max. He looked at Falcon.

"Whoa," said Max. "That was totally wack-a-mole."

"Whatever," said Falcon. "Let's get back to the dorm."

They walked down the path. "Hey. You think they're the
monsters, man?" said Max.

"I don't know," said Falcon. "I;ve been wondering who the monsters are. I think—" But then his voice fell silent. Looking up at Mossback Hal, he saw Megan Crofton, sitting in her window, looking down at them. She waved.

"Megan—" Falcon said. "She's okay."

"She is," said Max. "Hey, dude. You made out with her!"

"For like two seconds." He turned to his friend. "How come every time I kiss Megan, she turns invisible?"

"I don't know, man," said Max. "Bad luck, I guess. But I can tell you. I been in love with a ton of invisible people."

They climbed the stairs, walked down the hall. "See ya tomorrow," said Max. "Don't worry Falcon. We'll sort it all out."

"You think?" said Falcon. Max gave him the thumbs up sign.

As Falcon headed back to his room, he felt, for a moment, as if Max might be right. He often felt this after spending time in the Sasquatch's presence— that somehow the forces of kindness would triumph, that everything would roll into one happy go lucky lump. It was one of the things that Falcon liked most about Max. It was in the nature of Sasquatches to raise the spirits of others.

He opened the door to his room. Malcolm was sitting on the side of his bed, his face in his hand. Falcon could feel the energy in the room the second he walked in— Malcolm was the picture of despair.

"Hey," said Falcon. "Are you all right?"

Malcolm raised his head. He had a purple bruise on his face. His lip was bleeding.

"No, Falcon," he said in a softy, broken voice. "I don't think so."

7.

Puppets and Prisons

Malcolm hadn't changed his mind by the next morning, as they headed down to assembly.

"They were boasting about it," said Falcon to his roommate. The bruise on Malcolm's face had turned the color of an eggplant. "Max and I saw them. If we talk to the principal, we can make sure something gets done."

"I said no," Malcolm stated, firmly. "What's done is done."

"Why don't you fight back?"

"I just want to be left alone," said Malcolm.

"You think they're going to leave you alone? Gunk? Tripper?"

"Don't forget Muffy," said Malcolm. "She's the one who gave me this." He pointed to his cheek. "The other two held me down, while she kicked me."

"I can't believe this," said Falcon. They closed their door and headed down the stairs. Outside, the chapel bell was ringing.

"It wasn't the kicking that hurt," said Malcolm. "It was the words they said."

"Yeah?" said Falcon. He felt the heat in his dark eye smoldering. "What did they say?"

"What do you think?" said Malcolm. "They called me the kinds of names those people always use, when they're trying to hurt someone like me."

"Well, sticks and stones, Malcolm," said Falcon.

"What do you mean, sticks and stones?"

"You know that thing, about how sticks and stones can break your bones, but names—"

"Yeah well," said Malcolm. "The person who made up that rhyme never got names thrown at him. The names hurt worse than the kicks. The names show what people really think. And some of the things people think are just too depressing."

"I'm sorry," said Falcon.

"Yeah, well, you're next," said Malcolm. "If what you said was true about you and Max Parsons." He grinned. "I would have liked to have seen that, though. Max lifting Gunk off the ground. That would have been a-may-zing."

They entered the chapel and took their place in one of the pews. The chapel at Greenblud was one of the oldest buildings. It wasn't hard at all, as you sat in one of its pews, to imagine students sitting in this same place, a hundred years ago. Probably hearing the same announcements, too, Falcon thought.

"Good morning people," said Mrs. Houndstooth, the headmistress. "Settle down now. Settle down." She was a surprisingly young, stylish woman. She had a purse that hung by her side, and in the purse was a very small dog named Yap. Looking at her, Falcon found it hard not to think of Mrs. Redflint. You could say what you liked about Mrs. Houndstooth, but at least she never had fire coming out of her nostrils.

"Good morning. Let us begin this day with our traditional moment of silence and reflection."

"Yap," said Yap.

The students lowered their heads, and the room fell silent. Falcon liked this part of the day. He could feel the presence of the other students around him, each boy and girl thinking. It would be nice, Falcon thought, if the entire day could proceed with as much tranquility as this first moment.

He raised his head for a moment and looked to his right. Megan was seated across the aisle from him. She was looking at him. Megan smiled, uncertainly, then lowered her head again.

Falcon closed his eyes and thought about the night before. He remembered what it had felt like to kiss her. It was nice.

"Amen," said Mrs. Houndstooth, and the members of the student body said, "Amen." Some of them, anyhow.

"Yap," said Yap.

Then they all stood. After the morning moment of silence they sang the school alma mater.

Black and blue are our colors
And we raise them high above
In a tribute well deserved
To a school that we all love.
Sing her praises, sing her praises,

Til our hearts all over-flood

We are proud that we belong to the

School we call Greenblud.

"Please be seated," said Mrs. Houndstooth. "We have a few announcements today. As some of you know, there were tryouts last night for our musical group, the Bludstones. The final selections are Annie Hoptet, Timothy Sparkbolt, Max Parsons, and Malcolm Flynn."

"Rrr," said Sparkbolt.

"Please join me in congratulating them," said Mrs. Houndstooth. The students applauded.

"Yap," said Yap.

"Sparkbolts' first name is Timothy?" said Falcon.

"You didn't know that?" said Malcolm.

"Their first performance will be at the end of October, on Parents Weekend. We will look forward to welcoming all of your parents on October 31st."

"That's Halloween," said Mr. Scanappegio, the Dean of Students. He was a tired looking man in his early thirties, completely bald, with ugly black glasses.

"Yes, I'm afraid it is," said Mrs. Houndstooth.

Mr. Scanappegio didn't look happy about it. But Mrs. Houndstooth plunged onward. Finally, as you know, September is Diversity Month here at Greenblud, and as part of our program of special activities, I want to introduce to you the student who travelled farther to be part of our school than any other. She will tell

us about her home country, and the customs her people celebrate.
Will you please welcome, Olga Vzlynrßk?"

The students applauded lazily. There was a short pause. Then
Pearl's roommate stepped in from off stage. The student body
collectively gasped. Olga was wearing a spectacularly strange
costume. She wore a huge billowing skirt held up by a combination
of hoops and suspenders. Her blouse was made of leather and
affixed with crisscrossing leather straps. On her head was a helmet
with giant horns sticking out of either side, perhaps elk horns, or
moose. Her shoes were pointed and made of wood. In Olga's hands
was a great horn that appeared to have once been part of the head of
a giant ox.

"Is Olga," she said into the microphone. "Comes from
Vrzøzyzk. In Vest Zårnysk. Is landlocked. Brzzfldt Mountains to
North. Ügznazk Mountains to South and West. In East is Sea of
Lepers. Export is coal. Has King, King Rzpubzubszdub. Capital is
Bharf. Olga lives in Bharf."

The audience had begun to murmur softly.

"Has horn," Olga continued. She held up the thing she was
holding. "Not to blow unless danger. Blow horn, allies come to
help." She showed everyone the horn to make sure they saw it. It
had metal decorations all over it, and what looked like intricate
carvings at the bell end.

"Eats donkey," said Olga. "Traditional dish of Vrzøzyzkia. Donkey hit with sword. Boiled in fat. Once a year, national holiday. Feast of St. Heaugh."

The murmuring continued. It was getting louder.

"Does dance," Olga said. "Traditional dance of Vrzøzyzk on Feast of St. Heaugh. Dance of Large Maiden."

Olga took a moment to focus herself upon the task that now lay ahead. Then she began to dance, or perhaps gyrate would be a better word. She twisted back and forth, then she shouted something that sounded like, "Ruzz! Bup! Bup! Yakama-hakama-blatz!"

Then she slapped herself on the belly, raised both hands into the air, and did a complete backwards body flip. She landed, looked at her audience, then shouted again. "Ruzz! Bup! Bup! Yakama-hakama-blatz!" Olga nodded, as if pleased at her progress thus far, then moved forward and did not one, not two, but three full cartwheels. At the end of the last one she propelled herself into the air, landed on her two feet, raised her horn to her lips, and blew. It made a shocking sound, like a donkey braying.

"Za-zoo-za-zoo-za-zoo-ZAY!" shouted Olga, and then nodded. The dance was over.

"Is good," said Olga.

There was a moment of stunned silence, then the chapel burst into applause. Some members of the student body were laughing. But most of them were kind of awed by the spectacular dance of the Large Maiden.

Olga bowed, then walked off the stage.

"Wow," said Mrs. Houndstooth. She seemed astonished at what she had seen. "That was— uh—"

"Stupid," said a voice, that Falcon recognized as belonging to Tripper Murphy.

There was a chorus of derisive laughter.

"Who is it that has said this thing?" said another voice, which Falcon knew belonged to Pearl. "This one shall make himself known! And taste the cold steel of revenge, for the insult paid upon my friend!"

"Quiet," said Mrs. Houndstooth. "I am sure we are all very grateful to Olga for sharing with us her traditions. During the next few weeks, as we continue to celebrate Diversity Month, we will hear from many of you, and your own traditions. This is how we build a community. Through hearing each others' stories." She looked at Tripper, and some of the others, as if she could see through them. "Is there anyone who does not believe in building a better community?" The room fell silent. "Anyone?"

Mrs. Houndstooth's eyes flashed with anger.

"Because if there is anyone who does not believe in community, I would like to hear them speak now."

There was silence.

"We thank Olga for sharing. And we look forward to meeting Olga's parents on Parents' Weekend. We look forward to meeting all of your parents."

Yeah, Falcon thought. Everyone except mine. It made him mad to think that everyone in the room would have parents visiting that weekend, from stupid Tripper Murphy all the way down to Little Milton. Everyone except him.

"Yap," said Yap.

•

"Okay," said Quacky. He had arranged all the cards in front of him. "Now we can begin the quest."

"Rrr," said Sparkbolt.

"It confuses us with the rules," said Weems. "It needs to explain."

They were gathered in Quacky and Weems' room. Falcon and Max and Sparkbolt were there as well, along with Milton, Elaine, and Malcolm. There was also another boy named Tex, who was Max's lab partner in Bio. He was long and lanky, and wore a cowboy hat.

"We're playing Puppets and Prisons," said Quacky. "I'm the Prisonmaster. It's a live RPG. We start by pulling a card for our puppets."

They all reached forward and grabbed a card from the deck.

"Okay, so now we say what puppets we got."

"I'm, uh— a Chupakabra?" said Falcon.

"No way!" said Max, laughing.

"I don't see what's so funny about that," said Elaine.

"I am—" said Falcon. "La Chupakabra! The famous goat-sucker of Peru!"

Max laughed some more.

Quacky looked cross. "Chupakabras are from Mexico, actually," he said.

"Yeah, fine," said Max. "Let's go with that."

"What are you, Max?" said Quacky.

"Me? I got, uh— what? Office Worker?"

"Good," said Quacky. "Max's an O.W."

"I'm the Secret Swordsman," said Milton, a little embarrassed.

"I'm the Abominable Snowman," said Malcolm.

"Whoa, whoa, whoa," said Max. "How come everybody else is getting awesome monsters, and I got Office Worker? It's no fair."

"I can switch with you," said Milton fearfully. "I don't want to be the Secret Swordsman."

"No, no," said Quacky, a little irritated. "You have to take the puppet you draw. Then your puppet can puppi-volve, if you slay enough Dorks."

"Says I'm a Garbage Man," said Tex.

"Dude," said Max.

They read the rest of their cards. Elaine was a Wicked Witch. Weems was a Swamp Toad. Sparkbolt got Refrigerator Repairman.

It was a Friday night. Quacky and Weems' room was filled with bags of potato chips and soda. A single candle burned next to the deck of cards.

"Okay," said Quacky. "We go around clockwise. Garbage Man always goes first. Roll the twenty-seven sided die."

"This one?" said Tex, picking up one of the dice.

"No, no, no," said Quacky. "The other twenty-seven sided die. The red one. The black die is only for curses."

"Okey-dokey," said Tex. "Whatever y'all say."

"Haven't any of you ever played Puppets and Prisons before?" said Quacky.

"We have played something similar," said Weems. "In the past. When we were much younger. Much less alone."

"Fine, whatever," said Quacky. "Falcon, roll."

Tex rolled the die. It came up with the number nine.

"Nine," said Quacky. He checked a very large book next to him, a work almost the same size as an encyclopedia. "Okay. You enter a room. On the floor you see a dead body. What do you do?"

"What do I do?" said Tex. "I—uh— I look around, to see if the little ol' murderizer is still around. Cause if he is, I'm smashing him in the face with one of these here garbage can lids."

"You don't have garbage can lids," said Quacky, crossly. "You have to buy them from the armory."

"Where all's the armory?"

"You haven't gotten there yet!" shouted Quacky.

"Fine," said Tex. "So what do I do now. I'm looking around. Right?"

"You look around," said Quacky. "Okay, you're alone. There's no murderer there. Now what do you do?"

"What do I do?" said Tex. "I— I don't know. What choices ya got for me?"

"It searches the body for weapons," said Weems.

"You can do that," said Quacky. "Or you can summon another puppet to your squad. The bigger your squad, the more power you have. But the more sausages you'll need to sustain them."

"Okay," said Tex. "I'm eatin' sausages."

"You don't have sausages yet!" shouted Quacky.

"Where do I get sausages?"

"From the puppet grocery!"

"Okay, I'm going to the puppet grocery!"

"You can't go to the puppet grocery yet!" shouted Quacky. "You have to do something about the dead body."

"Okay, I kick it with my boot," said Tex.

"That's your choice?" said Elaine. "You're kicking the dead body?"

"Yeah, I kicked it. With my boot. You got a problem with that?"

Quacky was not happy with the way the quest was going. "Okay, roll." Tex rolled his die. "Twenty-six," he said. Quacky checked the reference book. "Okay, the body rolls over in response to your kick. What do you do now?"

"Uh—" Tex seemed confused. "I like, summon another member to my squad."

"Summoning," said Quacky. "Draw a card."

Tex pulled a card from the deck, and looked at it. "Says Magnifyin' Glass of Heat."

"There is a beam of light," said Quacky. "And a Wicked Witch appears." Everyone looked at Elaine. "That's you," said Quacky.

"Okay," said Elaine. "What do I do?"

"Roll," said Quacky. Elaine rolled the die. It game up thirteen. Quacky checked the reference book. He looked sad.

"Okay," said Quacky. "You're dead."

"Whoa whoa whoa," said Max. "She's dead, just like that?"

"Sorry," said Quacky.

"This game sucks," said Little Milton. "It's giving me a stomach-ache."

"We are enjoying it," said Weems.

"I hardly got to play at all!" said Elaine. Her eyes were tearing up. "It's not fair!"

"Garbage Man draws another card."

"It's okay, Laney," said Max. "You're still awesome." Elaine smiled, but a tear rolled down her cheek.

Tex drew a card, although he didn't seem very happy about it. "Says I got me a Vikin' Blast."

"Chupakabra enters on a Viking blast," said Quacky. Everyone looked at Falcon.

"Oh, yeah," he said. "Sorry. I forgot I'm a Chupakabra. I am— the famous goatsucker of Peru!"

"They're from Mexico," Quacky insisted.

"Why do you all keep sayin' that?" said Tex.

"I don't know," said Falcon. "Okay, now what."

"Roll," said Quacky. Falcon rolled a twenty. Quacky checked the book. "The body begins to glow," he said. "Then the glow fades. What do you do now?"

"I roll the body over," said Falcon. "So I can see who it is."

"Roll."

Falcon rolled. It came up twenty-seven.

"Twenty-seven," said Quacky. He consulted his volume once more. "Oh," he said. "It's James McNinch."

"Whoa whoa whoa," said Max. "That's the guy who died last semester? You're making him into a cartoon character now?"

"A puppet character," Quacky insisted. "It has to be someone we know. Who's dead."

"This isn't funny," said Elaine, standing up. "I'm not playing."

"We heard about this boy," said Weems. "It took its own life."

"He was murdered," said a voice from the door.

They all looked up to see who had spoken. There, framed in the doorway, was Judy Underhill.

"That's some nasty stuff to be sayin'," said Tex. "Boy wasn't murderized, Undy. I heard he just couldn't take it."

"Take what?" said Falcon.

"This is making my stomach hurt," said Little Milton.

"Can we please play our game?" said Quacky.

"It's not a game," said Malcolm. "It's real."

"Hey, it's not real," said Max. "I'm not an Office Worker. I'm like— a guy."

"You all need to be careful," said Judy Underhill. She looked frightened. "You need to look out for each other."

"Hey," said Max. He reached out and put his arms around the people next to him, which happened to be Elaine and Milton. "That's what we do! We look out for the people we love!"

"Is it?" said Judy.

"I am—" said Falcon. "La Chupakabra. The famous goatsucker of Peru! To my friends I pledge my sword!"

"Hey, this isn't a game," said Milton. "It's real."

"I know it," said Falcon.

Judy looked down the hallway, and her face looked fearful. There were footsteps. "Look out," she said. "Someone's coming."

"Who?"

But Judy had headed down the hallway. The footsteps drew near. Everyone in the room looked up at the door anxiously.

For a moment there was a terrible silence. Then Yap stepped into view. His tail pointed straight out from his rear end, and he raised one paw. Softly he growled.

"Yap," he said.

8.

The Slime

On a Saturday morning a few weeks later, Falcon was hurrying through a small wooded area near the main classroom building known as the Grotto. In the winters the Greenblud cross-country ski team used this area for practice, but here in the early autumn, it was mostly deserted. The leaves of the maples were turning red. A few drifted through the air as Falcon walked down the trail.

At last he arrived in the Outpost, the barn where Mr. Swishtail stood chewing hay in one corner.

"Sorry I'm late," said Falcon. "Were you worried about me?"

"Nay," said Mr. Swishtail.

"Dude," said Max The others monsters, in disguise, were all gathered there: Ankh-hoptet, Weems, Destynee, Merideath, Max, Pearl, Sparkbolt, and Megan. "I was just starting to get worried about you."

"I'm here," said Falcon. "I had to wait for Malcolm to head to practice. He's singing with the Bludstones."

"Sparkbolt skipping Bludstone practice," said Sparkbolt, then he cleared his throat. "Sparkbolt is skipping Bludstone practice." He cleared his throat again, concentrating. "I is skipping practice."

"Dude," said Max. "Look who's hooked on phonics."

"I is...practice..talking," said Sparkbolt.

"How wonderfully macabre," said Weems.

"My friends!" said Pearl. "We should begin the meeting! So that we may share with one another what we have learned!"

"Yes," said Falcon. "We've been here a month already. And from what I can see, we aren't any closer to finding the hidden monsters. Has anyone seen anything? Does anyone suspect anything?"

"That girl Muffy Chicago," said Merideath. "She's totally got vampire potential."

"Why do you say that," said Max. "Cause she's so annoying?"

"Ugh," said Merideath. "You wouldn't understand."

"I guess," said Max. "I tell you what though, Cheese and Pigpen could be Sasquatches. They're kind of big and awesome."

"And stupid," said Merideath.

"Guys," said Falcon. "Come on."

"My roommate, the Quacky," said Weems. "It is kind of worm-like. Yes, perhaps some kind of worm."

"Well, I for one shall say that my own roommate, the impressive Miss Olga, from the village of Bharf, might well be one of our kind! Although I would not wish to say what kind of our kind she must be!"

"Olga," said Merideath. "The dancing cow."

"You shall not speak of her with the tone of ridicule!" said Pearl. "To her I have sworn my friendship!"

"Yeah, come on Merideath. Remember? It's Diversity month."

"Diversity month," Merideath said, shaking her head. She looked around. "They want to see some diversity they should take a look around this barn."

"Hm," said Falcon. "It doesn't sound like we've made much progress. For all we know, the monsters could be anybody."

"Yeah, well," said Max. "It's not like you can just go up to someone and say, Dude are you a Sasquatch?"

"And they don't know themselves, what they are," said Megan.

"My first year at the Academy, I thought I was a vampire," said Destynee.

"Yeah, that's what you told everybody," said Merideath. "Until it turned out you were a disgusting enchanted slug."

"Yes, yes!" said Weems, in ecstasy. "Until she was revealed in all her beauty!"

"Stop it," said Destynee.

"What do we know about James McNinch?" said Megan. "The monster who died? No one wants to talk about him."

"Judy Underhill acts like she knows something," said Falcon. "But she won't say. She seems frightened, like if she says anything they will come for her."

"Sparkbolt learn thing," said Sparkbolt, then he cleared his throat again. "Sparkbolt learn a thing. I have a thing learned."

"Ugh, it's painful just to listen to you," said Merideath.

"What, Sparkbolt?" said Falcon. "What did you learn?"

"Him not dead," said Sparkbolt.

"What?" said Max. "He's not dead?"

"Dead, not dead," said Sparkbolt. "Not clear. Him disappear. That all. Maybe alive. Maybe not."

"Wait, who told you this?" said Max. "This sounds bogus."

"Gunk," said Sparkbolt.

"Wait, you mean Gunk the giant football dufus?" said Destynee. "I wouldn't trust anything that boy says."

"Him was friend. Told Sp— Told me. Before me see truth. Him mean. Not goodful."

"Please stop talking," said Meredeath, holding her hands over her ears. "I can't even."

"But that doesn't make any sense," said Falcon. "A student can't just vanish into thin air."

There was a pause. "Hey," said Destynee. "Where's Jonny?"

•

They left the old barn one at a time, each monster heading off in a different direction, in hopes they would not be seen traveling the campus as a group, and thus arousing suspicion. They'd broken up the meeting without much resolution, and with a growing fear that their mission was in danger of failure. On the way back to the dorm, however, Falcon heard footsteps behind him. At first he assumed that this was one of his friends from the meeting, but when he paused to see who it was, he found that Mr. Connelly and his wife were pushing a baby stroller along the leaf-strewn path.

"Falcon Quinn," said Mr. Connelly. "I don't think you've met my wife Rebecca."

"Hello," said the young woman. She had long black hair and red cheeks.

"Hello, ma'am," said Falcon, shaking hands with her.

"Falcon's in my English class," said Mr. Connelly.

"Is this your baby?" said Falcon.

"Yes," said Mrs. Connelly. "This is Angelique."

Falcon looked at the baby, who glowered back at him with a pair of dark black eyes and a deep set scowl. "Grrr," said the baby.

"She's collicky," said Mrs. Connelly.

"Falcon," said Mr. Connelly. "I don't suppose you're free this evening?" He cast an uncertain glance over at his wife. "If it's okay with Rebecca, perhaps you'd like to—join us? For dinner?"

"Grrr," said the baby.

"That's very nice of you," said Falcon. "But—"

"Oh, but you must come," said Mrs. Connelly. "I've heard so much about you."

"About me?" said Falcon.

"Well," said Mr. Connelly. "You are one of my best students."

"Please come," said Mrs. Connelly. "I'm making lasagna. Do you like lasagna?"

Falcon had been trying to come up with some good excuse for turning down the offer. But it was hard to say no to lasagna. "Okay," said Falcon. "That's awfully nice."

"7 O'clock, Radley Hall, top floor," said Mr. Connelly. "And bring a friend if you like!"

"Yes, bring a friend," said Mrs. Connelly. "We just love company."

"Grrrrr," said the baby.

•

When he got back to his room, Falcon heard voices. It sounded like two people were having an argument, but were trying to keep their voices down. One of the voices was Malcolm's. Something in him urged him to knock. It felt weird, knocking on his own door.

For a moment he wondered what it would be like if he himself opened the door and said, "What?"

"It's me, Falcon," he said, and then walked in. Malcolm and Quacky were sitting close together on Malcolm's bed. "Hi," he said. "I hope I'm not interrupting anything."

"Hi Falcon," said Malcolm. He still had a bruise on one cheek. "We're just talking."

"Malcolm wants to leave Greenblud," said Quacky. "I'm telling him that's stupid."

"I didn't say I was leaving," said Malcolm. "I just said I was thinking about it."

"Leaving," said Falcon. "Like, leaving leaving?"

Malcolm shrugged. "I don't know. I just can't take it."

"What can't you take?" said Falcon, although he knew the answer.

Quacky picked up a piece of paper and handed it to Falcon. "Someone put this under the door." Falcon looked at it. It read, Why don't you do everybody a favor and kill yourself. No one will notice.

"Oh my god," said Falcon. "But you have to report this. Tell Mrs. Houndstooth."

"We can't report it," said Malcolm. "That will only make them come at me harder."

Falcon felt something inside him beginning to smolder. His black eye felt like it was heating up. Against his shoulder blades he felt his hidden wings pressing against his bones.

"You can't leave," said Quacky. "That would be like letting them win."

"I don't want to wind up like John McNinch," said Malcolm.

"You won't wind up like him," said Quacky. "You have people that care about you." He reached out and rubbed Malcolm's shoulder.

Falcon took a deep breath, and the heat in his black eye cooled a little. He walked over to Malcolm and put his hand on his roommate's other shoulder. "You do," he added.

"Plus, if you leave it will mess up the Puppets and Prisons campaign. You're the only Abominable Snowman we got," said Quacky.

Malcolm nodded. "You guys are awesome," he said.

"Maybe you need to puppi-volve," said Quacky.

"Maybe you need to form a plan," said Falcon.

"What kind of plan?" said Malcolm.

"Look, we know who the bullies are. It's Tripper and Gunk and Muffy. We should give them a little of their own medicine."

"What are you talking about?" said Quacky.

"I don't know," said Falcon. "But they shouldn't be allowed to hurt people, just because they're different. Everybody gets to live their own life as whoever they are. Right?"

"You make it sound so easy," said Malcolm.

"I didn't say it was easy," said Falcon.

"Look, I appreciate you wanting to help," said Malcolm. "But you don't know what it's like. Being different. Having people wanting to hurt you, for no reason other than that you're who you are. Plus, if we play their game, that makes us as bad as they are, doesn't it?"

Falcon opened his mouth, then shut it. He wanted to shout at Malcolm, Dude, I'm a monster, raised up among humans. I think I know what it's like to feel different. But of course he couldn't say this. It was painful. He wanted to tell his friend, the burden isn't being different. The burden is having a secret.

Instead, he just nodded. "Malcolm," he said. "You and me? We have the same kind of eyes."

•

Just shy of seven o'clock, Falcon headed out the door to work his way over to the Connelly's. The plan was for him to swing by Megan's room first and for the two of them to head over to the faculty residence together, but as he walked across the quad, he ran into Destynee, who had tears running down her face. She was twisting her two hands together, as if she were trying to wash them clean of some terrible thing.

"Falcon," she said, out of breath. "You have to come with me. It's Jonny. He's sick."

"Jonny Frankenstein?" said Falcon. "Sick how?"

"He's coming all to pieces," said Destynee.

"What do you mean?" said Falcon. "How? Is he depressed?"

"No," said Destynee. "I mean he's actually coming all to pieces. I don't know what to do. He's— distintegrating?"

Falcon looked at his watch. "Okay," he said. "Let's go. Somebody needs to tell Megan, though. We're supposed to have dinner at the Connelly's house."

"She's already there," said Destynee.

Falcon followed her to the dorm where Jonny lived. The long hall on which his room was located was deserted for now, and Destynee gazed cautiously down its length before knocking on Jonny's door and slipping inside.

"Falcon," said Megan, rushing toward him, and throwing her arms around him.

"What's going on?" said Falcon, but even as he spoke the words he took in the scene before him. Jonny lay on the bed, his face illuminated with a strange expression, equal measures melancholy and nobility. Unfortunately, his head was the only part of his body on the bed. His arms had fallen off and rolled onto the floor; the hands were still clenching and unclenching, as if trying to grasp hold of something that even now was slipping away. The rest of his torso was wandering around the room, blind, crashing into the wall. As Falcon watched, it slammed into the wall near the window and fell to the floor. The legs detached from the torso and rolled around the floor like a pair of trunks in a log-rolling contest.

"Jonny," said Falcon. "What's happening to you?"

"I told you when we met," said Jonny. "I'm just a piece of junk."

"Don't say that!" shouted Destynee, sitting down on the bed, and touching the cheeks of the head. "You're not."

"You're disintegrating," said Falcon. "Why?"

"Oh, Falcon," said Jonny's head. One of his arms drug itself closer to the bed. "I told you. I was just an experiment. I did okay, for as long as I lasted."

"We're putting you back together," said Destynee. "We're going to save you!"

"You need to save yourselves," said Jonny. "You don't have much time left."

"Jonny, why is this happening now? Tell me," said Falcon.

"You remember," said Jonny's head. It seemed as if he was slowly diminishing in power. His voice was getting softer. "At the end of the battle of Monster Island. Merideath and those vampire girls cornered me. I had to— give in to them. To save the rest of you."

"Give in?" said Megan. "What are you talking about?"

"They bit me," said Jonny. "They gave me the vampire's kiss."

"Wait," said Destynee. "You're a vampire now? Is that what you're saying?"

"I'm not," said Jonny. "That kiss doesn't work on... the inhuman."

"Inhuman?" said Destynee. "Who said you're inhuman?"

Jonny's head, resting against the pillow, laughed softly. "No one needed to say anything," he said.

"Falcon," said Megan urgently. "Do something."

"What can I do?" said Falcon. He felt something pressing against his shoulder blades.

"Use your healing eye," said Destynee. "You can save him! Use your blue eye beam thing! You have to!" Jonny's hands, at the end of his detached arms, spread their fingers, as if begging for something that could not be given.

"I can't use the eye without reverting to monster form," said Falcon. "It'll place us all in danger."

"Oh, Falcon," said Megan. "Do it. Please. You have to save him."

"It's too late," said Jonny. "I can't be put back together. It's the vampire's kiss. All my pieces have gone dark. The thing that holds them together is gone. I'm just— a bunch of pieces. I'm done for."

"What holds you together?" said Destynee. "Tell me. I'll bring it to you." She stroked his face. "Please, Jonny. Tell me. I can't live with you... in pieces."

Jonny looked up at her. "Don't you know what holds me together, Destynee?" He smiled a weak smile. "You know. Of course you know. My maker didn't have it for me. But I found it in the world. Among my friends, and the people that I've known. The force that has kept me whole." His left eye bulged as it stared intently as Destynee, and then, suddenly, popped out of his face and rolled onto the floor like a ping pong ball. "But when that's gone...." Now his other eye bulged and swelled and, finally, popped. The face upon the pillow closed its eyelids.

"Jonny, no!" shouted Destynee. "I love you, you stupid Frankenstein. Don't you know that? I've always loved you!"

The arm crawling around on the floor grabbed one of the eyes in its fingers and held it up to face Destynee. She looked at it, her heart full. "Can you still see me?" she said to the eye. "I'm here, Jonny. I've always been here!" Tears brimmed over her eyelids and began to roll down her face.

"When I go," said Jonny. "It's just one death in a thousand. A million, maybe. But when love is gone. It's a million deaths in... in one...."

They looked at the eye, and watched as the life slowly drained out of it.

"Jonny!" Destynee shouted. "No!"

They were all weeping now, mourning their loss. But even as they sat there on the edge of the bed, there came a sound from the hallway, a sound of the approaching footsteps of something very large and heavy.

Falcon and Megan and Destynee stared at the door, wondering what this new devilry might be. There was a shuffling and a growling, coming right up to the door, and then a momentary silence.

And then the door burst open, and a tremendously revolting creature was suddenly upon them. It was nine feet tall, almost twice

as tall as Megan, and its skin—if that's the right word for it—
consisted of a moving yellow slime that contained all sorts of chunks
and wrinkles. Two basketball sized eyes were perched the top of its
moving mound of gelatinous goop, and they moved independently of
each other, taking in the room in which the creature had entered. It
had no arms or legs, although certain parts of the giant glistening
slime seemed to move forward with the intention of reaching out and
taking hold of things.

Megan and Destynee both screamed, and screamed loudly. But
Falcon planted himself between the creature and Jonny's bed, and
pointed at it. "We are your friends!" he said evenly. "You have
nothing to fear here!"

Part of the thing oozed forward and wrapped itself around one
of Jonny's legs. In a moment the leg had been absorbed into the
shining yellow glop. Another part of the creature branched out and
slimed over one of Jonny's arms. A third gushed over one of
Jonny's eyeballs.

"Stand back," said Falcon, but in response to this the creature
only made a deep gurgling sound. He wasn't certain but it sounded
like it was laughing.

Deep inside the creatures slime, Falcon could see—or thought
he could see—pieces of other creatures. There was another pair of
eyes, and a human hand. There were objects in the slime as well—
somebody's shoe, a cell phone, a ring. For a single moment,
bubbling to the surface, Falcon saw a face, and Falcon thought, John

McNinch. The face looked at Falcon, and said, Help me. Then, just as swiftly, it sank back into the moving, churning glop.

"Falcon," said Megan, pointing to the bed.

A tentacle of slime had oozed over to the pillow, absorbing Jonny's head into its sizzling, stinking foam. Other arms shot out of the creature and consumed all that remained of Jonny. It made the awful gurgling, laughing sound once more, and then it retreated back to the door and closed it shut behind it with a loud bang. Falcon and Megan rushed after it, but the door had been jammed, and it took a moment to get it open again.

When they stepped into the hallway, they found it deserted. There was no sign of the monster anywhere. They looked up and down, checked the stairwell. Whatever it was had vanished.

"Well," said Falcon. "Looks like we found one of the monsters."

"Oh Falcon," said Megan, tears running down her face. She put her arms around him. "That was horrible. What are we going to do?"

Destynee just sad on Falcon's bed, crying into her hands. "You're not a piece of junk," she said. "You're not."

There were footsteps on the stairs, and the door to the staircase opened. There was Weems, all in black. He paused for a moment, looking at Falcon and Megan and Destynee.

"Weems," said Megan. "We saw one of the monsters. It came for Jonny."

"Jonny Frankenstein?" said Weems, his pale bulbous eyes growing even larger in their sockets. "What's become of this one?"

"He's gone," said Destynee.

"Gone, is he?' said Weems. He seemed uncertain. "Gone?"

Destynee nodded, and the tears rolled down her face.

Weems stood upon the threshold of the room, almost afraid to enter. "Oh my Beloved," he said. "I am so sorry."

"Don't call me that!" shouted Destynee. "You're the last person I want to see right now!"

"I know it," said Weems, his eyes falling to the floor. "I've been so—hungry all the time. It's is not your fault, the hunger that I bear."

Destynee just sat there on the bed, touching the pillow.

"It said," said Weems, "it was a piece of junk. But it wasn't. It was the shiniest gold." He sat down on the bed next to her. "Who would take him?" he said. "Who?"

"It was a slime monster," said Megan. "It came in here and stole his body."

Weems eyes grew smaller. "We will find this slime," he said. "We will find it and take the revenge."

"I don't want revenge," said Destynee. "I just want Jonny back."

"Weems, can you look out for Destynee for a little bit? Megan and I have to go to the Connelly's house."

"Oh my god," said Megan, swaying back and forth a little. "I forgot about the stupid Connelleys. We can't be expected to go now, can we? After what's happened?"

"Nobody knows what happened, except us," said Destynee. "We have to keep it secret, until we can find that monster. And the others. That's the mission."

Weems nodded thoughtfully "It is very brave," he said.

"I think I ought to go to the Connellys," said Falcon. "There's something weird about them. We ought to learn more. You don't have to come if you don't want, Megan."

"No, I'll go," she said. In a smaller voice she said, "We're still on a mission."

Falcon turned to Destynee. "You're okay here?"

Weems looked at Falcon, then put his arm on Destynee's back. "I will take care of this one." He sighed. "So crunchy."

"All right then," said Falcon. "Let's go."

Falcon and Megan headed down the stairs and outside. They'd only taken a few paces when Megan had to stop, lean against the wall of Mossback Hall.

"Are you all right?" said Falcon.

"No," said Megan. "How could I be all right? I just saw Jonny Frankenstein disintegrate, and then a slime monster ate him. I'm the opposite of all right."

"I don't mean that," said Falcon. "I mean—"

"Falcon," said Megan. "I made a mistake." Her eyes shimmered with tears. "I'm not making it again."

"You mean—letting Muffy pressure you like that? Drinking that stuff?"

"That was wrong, I know. I'm not doing that again," said Megan. "But that's not the mistake I mean."

Falcon looked at her, hard. "So what do you mean?"

"Don't you know?" said Megan. Her hair lifted from her shoulders, and blew around her face.

"Maybe— that you wish you hadn't kissed me. That time. You regret that."

"Falcon," said Megan. Her hair was blowing all around her. Her eyes were shining. "I'll never regret that. Ever." She leaned forward and touched his cheeks with her hands. "I'm just sad what happens after."

"What do you mean," said Falcon. "What happens after?"

Megan looked at Falcon with her sad eyes, then kissed him. He felt her lips upon his. "Faaa," she said.

There was a gust of wind, and Megan vanished.

Falcon looked around him. A pile of leaves blew in a soft circle. A flag on the flagpole fluttered.

"Wait," he said. "What?"

•

Falcon was late to the Connelly's apartment in Radley Hall, which was at the opposite end of the Greenblud campus from Mossback. He might have made up some of the difference by

running from to the teachers' house, but he didn't feel like it.
Mostly what he wanted to do was lie down on the grass and cry, or
scream, or both. He had seen three terrible things within the space
of a few minutes. He had seen one of his best friends disintegrate.
He had seen a slime-monster appear out of nowhere, absorb the
pieces, and then vanish. And finally, he had seen the girl that he
loved, Megan, dissipate into wind.

Somehow it didn't put him in the mood to have dinner with his
English teacher.

It would have been natural enough for Falcon to be haunted by
the sight of Jonny's bodiless head, lying on its pillow, lamenting
what he thought was the absence of love in his life. And no one
would have been surprised if, in thinking of that slime, Falcon's
heart had been filled with terror and sadness. Even now the memory
of the pieces of other students, and their lost belongings, floating in
the slime, was hard to forget.

But as he walked toward the Connelly's, mostly what he thought
about was Megan.

Jonny, he said to himself. What am I going to do about her?

He thought about the way Jonny used to sit on his bed back at
the Academy for Monsters and play his guitar, plugged into the
amplifier in his neck. He thought about the lightning bolts Jonny
could summon, when he was in great need, the forking electricity
that could surge from his commanding hands. It's just this thing I
can do, he liked to say.

Jonny, he thought, as he entered Radley Hall and climbed the stairs to the fourth floor. Why would you ever think that you were unloved, when you were constantly surrounded by your friends?

But even as he thought this, Falcon knew the answer: that sometimes people were blind to the love that others felt for them— or, even worse, that even when people knew that they were loved, it didn't diminish the sadness they carried. And sometimes, it wasn't the love of the people at hand you craved; it was the love of people who had walked away, just as Falcon's parents had walked away from him; just as the scientist who had built Jonny Frankenstein had walked away from his creation.

He climbed the stairs to the Connelly's, and then paused before the door. I really don't want to be here he thought. I would rather be anywhere else.

He knocked.

"Ah, Falcon!" said Mr. Connelly, opening the door. "Splendid!"

Within a few minutes of walking into the Connelly's apartment, Falcon could see that the couple had given up even pretending to clean the place up. At one time, he imagined, it had been the kind of place you'd expect from an English teacher— walls of books, a grand piano, comfortable leather chairs. But a vast tide of baby things had swept through the house. There were blocks and Legos and stuffed animals and tangled baby blankets on the floor. In one corner was some sort of baby-swing; from a door-jamb was suspended some sort of baby-bouncer on a bungee cord. There were disposable diapers and bottles of formula and sippy cups and jars of baby food. A few stray Thomas the Tank engine figures were scattered on the floor next to a plastic fire truck.

In the midst of the room, looking like the lord of a medieval fiefdom, was baby Angelique, sitting thoughtfully and holding a tiny plastic pitchfork in one hand. She looked at Falcon with dark, knowing eyes. Falcon wasn't certain, but the baby appeared to smile when she gazed upon him.

"Hah hah hah," said baby Angelique, staring at Falcon. "Hah hah hah."

"Hi Falcon!" called Mrs. Connelly from the kitchen. She came out wearing a fluffy apron.

"Hello, Mrs. Connelly," he said.

"We're glad you're here," said Mr. Connelly, and winked at Falcon. Falcon thought, wait, you're winking? What's to wink about?

Mrs. Connelly looked at Falcon thoughtfully, as if she were seeing, somehow, into his soul. She raised one hand to her face.

"Are you all right, dear?" she said. Falcon thought, Dear?

"I'm fine," said Falcon, hoping that the horrors of the last hour or two were not visible upon his face.

"Hah hah hah," said the baby. She pointed at Falcon.

"Please," said Mr. Connelly. "Be seated." Falcon looked around but he wasn't entirely sure where to sit. "Ah," said Mr. Connelly. "Sorry about the mess." He shoved a pile of baby pants and newspapers and baby bottles onto the floor. "We've been a bit overwhelmed since Angelique was born."

"Speak for yourself," said Mrs. Connelly.

"I was speaking for myself," said Mr. Connelly, a bit tersely. "Who else would I be speaking for."

"How old is she?" said Falcon.

"Just a month old!" said Mr. Connelly. "A month old tomorrow!"

Falcon thought about this. "And— she's already sitting up— and crawling around?" He wasn't certain, but this seemed more than a little swift.

"She's very advanced!" said Mrs. Connelly.

Mr. Connelly nodded. "That she is," he said. He didn't seem happy about it.

"Grrr," said the child.

"She's really cute," said Falcon.

"Do you really think so?" said Mrs. Connelly. Falcon hoped that she couldn't tell that he was lying. In fact, the child looked a lot like one of those gargoyles you might see perched atop a ruined cathedral.

"Sure," said Falcon.

The baby pointed at Falcon and said, "Hah hah hah."

"Oh, I'm so glad you like her," said Mrs. Connelly. Falcon thought, why do you care what I think about your ugly baby? Or, for that matter anything?

Mrs. Connelly went back into the kitchen, and a moment later Falcon heard the sound of pots and pans banging around.

"Mrs. C. is making lasagna," her husband said, and sighed.

"Great," said Falcon.

"Well listen, Falcon. I'm delighted you've joined us tonight." The man ran his hand through his longish brown hair. "I wanted you to know I'm pleased with the progress you're making in English. You're a good writer. Did you know that? You are."

"Thanks, Mr. Connelly."

"I think you have a real talent," said the man. He looked into Falcon's eyes, and held them for a moment. "You have a very — what can I call it? Insightful view of the world."

"I don't know about that," said Falcon.

"I think you do," said Mr. Connelly. "I hope you'll keep writing. Writing stories. I think it's through telling our stories that we come to understand ourselves."

"How do you mean?" said Falcon. Baby Angelique was slowly crawling toward them.

"I mean, life is chaos, mostly," said the teacher. "But when you tell a story about your life, you bring your story meaning. Sometimes you don't know what it is that's happened to you until you try to figure out the narrative."

Mrs. Connelly came out into the room again. She'd taken off the apron.

"Weren't you going to bring a friend, dear?" she said. "I thought you said Miss Crofton was joining us."

"She— wasn't feeling well," said Falcon.

Mr. Connelly and his wife exchanged a quick glance.

"Nothing too serious, I should hope?" said Mrs. Connelly.

"I don't know," said Falcon.

"Hah hah hah," said the baby, standing up on its legs and putting its hands on the cushion of the couch.

"Well hello," said Mr. Connelly. He lifted the baby into his arms, and a smile of remarkable happiness crept over his face. "And hows my little angel?" he said.

"Grrr," said the baby.

"Uh-oh," said the teacher. He sniffed, and wrinkled his nose. "Will you excuse me?"

"Is she poopy?" said Mrs. Connelly.

Mr. Connelly nodded. "She's poopy all right." The man stood, the baby in his arms, and left the room. That left Falcon in the room with Mrs. Connelly. She was looking at him intently. She had a big head of poofy curly hair, and a long nose. A pair of small glasses were balanced on the bridge.

"Are you a teacher here too, Mrs. Connelly?" he said.

"Oh, no," she said. "I'm just— well, I guess I'm kind of a housewife." She laughed. Sensing Falcon's uncertainty, she said, "Forgive me for laughing. But housewife is the last thing I expected to wind up. It wasn't what I was trained for. But since I got pregnant mostly I've been taking care of myself. And since the baby

was born, it's all I can do to feed Angelique. She's a very
demanding baby."

"What were you trained for?" said Falcon.

"Oh, all sorts of things," said Mrs. Connelly. Falcon noticed
that the room was now beginning to smell strongly of the cooking
lasagna. It made his mouth water. "Originally I was going to be a
musician, actually."

"Really?" said Falcon. "What do you play?"

"Piano," she said, looking over at the instrument in the corner,
and then back at Falcon. "Here, I'll play you something. Do you
like Mozart?"

She made her way over to the piano, then began to play. He
thought of his mother, Vega, who had welcomed him to the Island of
the Guardians by playing ragtime on a piano in her house by the sea.
He had thought, at the time, that he was going to begin a new life
with her. But then she'd shown her true colors, as a cruel and
monster-hating Guardian. In the end he'd had to flee from her,
afraid of what she might do next. His fears had not been unjustified,
either. It was Vega, of course, who had trapped Megan in the
entangling sails.

"What is it?" said Mrs. Connelly, suddenly, looking at him.

"Oh, nothing," said Falcon.

"I know enough to know nothing is something. Come on, spill
the beans." She shot a glance toward the hallway through which her

husband had gone. "I won't tell my husband. Or anyone, for that matter. It'll just be our secret."

There was something about the woman that made Falcon feel as if he could almost trust her, although in his hearts he knew better. "I was just thinking about some of my friends," he said.

"Oh? What about them?"

"About the trouble people get themselves in to. And how you can't help people no matter how much you love them."

Mrs. Connelly nodded. "Well, that's very true," she said. "You can't stand between the people you care about and all the trouble in the world. That doesn't mean you shouldn't try, of course. But sometimes when you try to help people it must makes things a thousand times worse."

"So what do you do?" said Falcon. "You can't just abandon people to their demons."

"No, you can't," said Mrs. Connelly. "You have to try to be loving, I think. Even if the people you love are doomed."

She looked at Falcon with such an intense look that for a moment he felt that she was seeing into his secret hearts. Does she know, he wondered? Does she know that I'm actually an angel? And that, as an angel, I'm kind of a failure? I'm supposed to be capable of all this good in the world, but I don't know how to bring it about.

"Doomed?" said Falcon, and as he said the word, his voice broke.

At that moment, the fire alarm in the kitchen went off. Mrs. Connelly said, "Oh!" and leaped to her feet and ran out of the room. He heard her fumbling around with the fire alarm for a moment, pulling out its batteries, until the shrill alarm stopped. For a second everything was quiet.

Then he heard a voice. "Hah hah hah," it said, and baby Angelique walked— not crawled, but walked— into the room.

The baby walked toward right toward the place where Falcon was sitting and then pointed at him. Her eyes glowed red, like they were filled with fire.

"Doomed," said the baby.

9.

The Big Picture

"And so," said Pearl. "I shall sit behind the controls of this automotive transportation invention, and operate it in a manner that shall propel it forward, into the heart of the nation!"

"Do you have your permit?" Mr. Sheetz, the driving instructor said. At Greenblud, he taught French. He turned to the student in the back seat. "Falcon? Olga? Muffy? Do we all have our permits?"

"The documentation you have requested is here upon my person!" shouted Pearl. "I am now prepared now to engage upon this adventure!"

"Does she always shout everything?" said Muffy. "Its so boringly boring."

"Has fire," said Olga. "Is good."

"I've got my permit," said Falcon, holding up the paper he'd received from the State of New Hampshire.

"Ha ha," said Muffy, whipping out a white iPhone, and tapping away on it.

"Is funny?"

"I'm tweeting," said Muffy.

"Like the songbirds of the forest," said Pearl. "You shall know the music of the world in which we dwell!"

"All right, Pearl," said Mr. Sheetz. He was a man with red hair and a jowly neck. "Put the vehicle into Drive, and let's move forward into traffic."

"I shall engage the controls!" shouted Pearl. "And together, we shall move forward in this motorized contraption! As friends!"

"Let's keep our voice down," said Mr. Sheetz, and concentrate on driving. "Remember, Pearl, Get the Big Picture! That's the most important thing! Get the Big Picture!

"My concentration is honed like the point of a sword," said Pearl. "It has been sharpened by the loyalty I bear in my heart! With this none shall interfere! And thus shall this Big Picture come into being at last!"

"Ha ha," said Muffy.

"Is laughing," said Olga. Because Olga was so large, the back seat which she and Falcon and Muffy shared was tight quarters.

"Can you move over," whined Muffy. "I can't breathe."

"In Bharf," said Olga. "Lived in Squwuzz. Many persons."

"Skwuzz?" said Muff. "Seriously? That's the name of your home town?"

"Town was Bharf," said Olga. "Squwuzz was hut. Dirt floor. Fire pit for eating. Charred squirrel."

"What century was this you lived in?" said Muffy. "It sounds disgusting."

"Put on your turn signal, Pearl," said Mr. Sheetz.

"Is poor country," explained Olga. "No cars. Field of mud, many donkey. Family strong. Poor family, strong bone."

"Dis-gusting," said Muffy. "Charred squrriel? Seriously?"

"Like chicken it tastes."

"Slow, slow," said Mr. Sheetz. Pearl was approaching an intersection with a traffic light. She sped up as the light turned yellow. Another car honked its horn. "I said slow! Yield to the oncoming traffic!"

"It is not to yield that I was born to this world!" shouted Pearl. "It was to triumph, against all that would interfere!"

"Stay in your lane!" shouted Mr. Sheetz.

"Is not disgusting," said Olga. "Is noble!"

"Ugh," said Muffy. "I'd rather die than live in Barf."

"Is Bharf! Not Barf! Bharf! Bharf! Bharf! "

"Pearl, slow down, now," said Mr. Sheetz. He pulled a polka dot handkerchief out of his jacket pocket and mopped his head with it. Pearl honked the horn at a cement mixer that pulled out in front of her.

"Who is it that would impede our progress?" Pearl shouted. She swerved into the passing lane and floored it. "To him we shall respond with our laughter and contempt!"

"Pearl!"

"Bharf, Barf," said Muffy. "it's disgusting."

"Does not insult Vrzøzyz!" said Olga, turning to Muffy and clamping her huge fat fingers across Muffy's throat. "Does not speak at all!" Muffy turned red and the veins in her neck budged out.

A large truck swerved into view around a far curve and began to hurtle toward them. Pearl was still passing the cement mixer. The truck, which was marked HORSES, flashed its lights and honked its horn. They were approaching a railroad crossing.

"Pull over!" shouted Mr. Sheetz. "Pull over!"

"There is no place for this pulling!" noted Pearl. "We can only increase our speed! And face our destiny with courage!"

"Aaak," said Muffy, still choking.

Falcon felt his dark eye smoldering in his skull. They seemed only seconds away from disaster. Then, just as they crossed the railroad tracks, Pearl turned the wheel hard to the left, and the car bumped onto the rails. The truck marked HORSES blasted past them, barely missing them, as the cement mixer honked its horn.

"Aaak," said Muffy, turning the color of beets.

Now they were on the railroad tracks, bouncing up and down upon the ties. "And so!" shouted Pearl. "By surprise we find ourselves upon the tracks of locomotion!"

"Stop," said Falcon to Olga.

"Stop," said Mr. Sheetz to Pearl.

"Is stopping," said Olga. Mr. Sheetz wriggled over to the drivers side of the car and jammed his foot down upon the brake. The car shuddered to a violent halt.

"Everyone, out," said Mr. Sheetz. The doors of the car swung open, and everyone fell out onto the tracks, except for Muffy, who lay in the back seat gasping for breath.

"What is wrong with you!" shouted Mr. Sheetz. "You almost killed us, young lady!" He mopped his head with the polka-dotted handkerchief once more.

"And yet we have triumphed!" observed Pearl. "Victorious we stand over all of those who would stand against us, or our friends!"

Muffy staggered out of the car, tears streaming down her face.

"You're a bully," said Muffy to Olga. "You hurt me."

"Is real bully," said Olga, pointing at Muffy. "Insults everyone!"

"It's not my fault your country is disgusting!"

"Shut up," said Falcon. His dark eye was heating up. "Everyone—" He felt his wings pressing against his shoulder blades. In a moment they were going to pop out again and rip through his shirt. It was exactly what had happened with Megan that night, except that then he'd been full of happiness and delight, and now he was angry and scared.

"Country disgusting," said Olga. "People noble and true."

"And so!" said Pearl, standing at Olga's side. "We shall be friends!"

"I have to go," muttered Falcon, and ran from the train tracks and into the woods.

"Wait," said Mr. Sheetz. "Falcon! Come back here!"

"Where's he running off to?" said Muffy.

"Everyone remain calm," said Mr. Sheetz. "Everyone remain…"

But at that moment, a loud horn sounded. From around the curve before them appeared a freight train, its bright headlight stabbing into view. The horn sounded again.

"Oh dear," said Mr. Sheetz.

The train plowed straight into the car as Mr. Sheetz, Olga, Muffy, and Pearl watched. It was as if the car itself had only been held together with the rust upon its body, for the car exploded in every direction. One minute it was sitting there on the tracks; the next the train had smashed through it and every last piece of metal that had once been part of the car was flying through the air. The pieces rained down around them.

"And so," said Pearl to Mr. Sheetz. "This Big Picture has now emerged for us at last!"

•

Falcon ran through the forest. Through the trees behind him, he heard the horn of the oncoming train, and the explosion as it ran into Mr. Sheetz's car. He kept running. He felt his wings pressing against his shirt, and then ripping through the material. He kept running. A bright halo shone around his head. In the distance he heard people calling his name.

Falcon ran faster, then flapped his wings once, twice, and was airborne. He watched as the ground receded. Before him was the limb of an old oak tree, and he raised his wings and landed on it. He heaved a sigh. This, he thought, is not good.

His twin hearts beat in his chest. Calm, he thought. I have to calm down. That's the only way I'm going to revert back to human form. I just have to concentrate.

And so he closed his eyes and counted to ten, slowly, focussing on his breathing. In and out, in and out. He felt his wings slowly settling back onto his shoulder blades, retracting and withdrawing. The halo that hovered above him slowly faded.

Just as he had almost reverted back to human, Falcon heard
voices. They're going to wonder what happened to me, Falcon
thought. They're going to wonder how I got up here. He looked
around but it wasn't immediately clear how to get down.

"Dude I can't," said a voice. He looked toward the direction in
which he had come, imagining that he would see Muffy, or Pearl, or
even Mr. Sheetz. Instead, to his surprise, he saw Gunk and Tripper
Murphy, deep in an argument. He realized, with some shock, that he
was still on the grounds of Greenblud Academy, on the outer
perimeter of the bird sanctuary, a large and mostly undeveloped tract
of land behind the main campus, beyond The Grotto. Given the
ridiculous series of events in the car, Falcon had somehow imagined
that they were miles and miles from campus. But he was really not
all that far from home, if home was the word for the place he had
been living.

"Of course you can," said Tripper. The two boys walked
through the woods and paused at the base of the tree. "You have to."

"That's easy for you to say, man," said Gunk. "You're not the
one who has to do it."

"I'm the one who'll never be class president," said Tripper.
"I'm the one who has to let that lunatic win."

The boys stopped beneath the oak tree in which Falcon was
sitting. "You ran a crappy campaign, Tripper," said Gunk. "That's
not my fault."

"How can anybody take her seriously?" said Tripper. "The way she orders people around!"

"You order people around," said Gunk.

"For a reason," said Tripper. "I know what has to be done. She's just—I don't know, there's something creepy about her. There's something creepy about a lot of the new kids. Did you notice that?"

"Freaks," said Gunk. "The bunch of them. Hoptet. That girl Megan who rooms with Muffy. That kid Weems? And what's with that girl Pearl and her rooommate Olga? It's like we're going to high school in an asylum."

"And people love them!" said Tripper. "That's what I don't get! They love these weirdoes, while people with real school spirit get shoved aside, and humiliated!"

"They're a bunch of bullies, all of them," said Gunk.

"They are," said Tripper. "But we'll show them. With the Bucket Project. It's perfect."

"So who are we taking down?"

Tripper thought. "We can't take down all of them. But Hoptet, for one. And that Malcolm. Max Parsons. And Sparkbolt. They're all in that singing group. We need to take them out, those four."

Gunk looked thoughtful.

"What," said Tripper. "You're having second thoughts?"

"It's too bad about Sparkbolt," said Gunk. "He had potential."

"Yeah, but he made his choice. He sided with Cheese and Max and Pigpen that day, remember? You don't get a second chance."

"Okay," said Gunk. "Sparkbolt too."

"On parents weekend," said Tripper. "During their little concert. We'll give them the bucket."

Footsteps approached through the woods. "Sssh," said Gunk. "Someone's coming. Come on, let's go." The two boys looked at each other with evil grins, then rushed down the path that led back to Greenblud.

A moment later, Olga and Pearl walked through the woods toward the same spot. They paused.

"Is good the Muffy returned with the Sheetz," said Olga. "Time spent with this one makes sickness in foot."

"It is true, the things you have said!" shouted Pearl. "This one, this Muffy, she does not behave as one would expect, of one's sworn companion."

"Olga has new companion," said Olga. "Olga does not know how."

Pearl looked at her roommate curiously. "I am not entirely sure I have understood what you intend? What is this meaning?"

"Is Olga," said Olga. "From Bharf. No friends, until Pearl, from Peru. Now one friend. Is Pearl. Is good."

"Indeed!" said Pearl. "It is good that we have sworn our friendship! Together we shall defeat all our enemies!"

Olga looked thoughtful. "Pearl of Peru does not tell all her secrets," she said softly. "Olga does not require the knowing of all. But Pearl of Peru must know. Olga suspects."

"What is this?" said Pearl. "Of what do you speak? Surely there shall be no secrets between us!"

"Always secrets," said Olga. "Is nature. No one is known in full. Olga respects Pearl of Peru. But Peal must know that Olga has eyes. Olga sees."

"And what is this you see?" said Pearl. Falcon thought he could feel a slight uneasiness creeping into her voice.

"Is not what she seems," said Olga. "Is other."

She's got to stop this, Falcon thought. Knowing Pearl, there was no way she would lie to her sworn friend. If Olga asked her if she was really a monster, Pearl would confess.

"My friend!" said Pearl. "Surely you do not doubt my honor, and my courage! We have sworn allegiance to each other!"

"No doubt courage or honor. Pearl has strength. But Olga sees."

"And this that you see—" said Pearl. "What is this thing? Shall it not be named?"

Falcon did not see that he had any choice. "Ugh— ugh— ugh— " he said. And jumped out of the tree.

He landed on Olga, which, owing to her size, was a little like landing on a very soft chair. Still, his downward plummet knocked Olga to the ground, and Pearl, already in a heightened frame of mind, reacted as if her friend were under attack.

"En guarde!" said Pearl, and in that moment she began to flicker. For a single moment, she transformed back into La Chupakabra, her tiny wings lifting her into the air, and her poisonous stinger piercing through the back of her pants. "I am—" she shouted, "I am—"

"You're fine," said Falcon. "It's only me."

Olga, who had had her face pressed against the ground, slowly sat up, and at that same moment, Pearl transformed back into her human simulacrum.

"Is what?" said Olga.

"Sorry," said Falcon. "I fell."

"From the branches above you have plummeted to the earth!" shouted Pearl. "Before we were only two! But now we are three!"

Olga stood up. "Comes from tree?" she said.

Falcon nodded. "Sorry," he said. "I kind of freaked out back there. When we almost had the car accident. I'm all right."

Olga looked at Falcon, and then back at Pearl. She nodded. "Is good," she said. "Was making mistake. Mistake has been stopped."

"There is no such thing as a mistake!" Pearl said. "When it comes to friends!"

"Does not need to be said," said Olga. "Understands in heart. Some truth best unspoken. Heart knows. Is good."

"You're both all right?" said Falcon.

"I am better now than at any time!" said Pearl.

They began to walk down the path, back toward Greenblud High. "Is friend. But driver," Olga said. "Pearl bad."

"It is not through our skills operating this vehicle that one's honor is measured!" said Pearl.

"Is good," said Olga.

•

At Morning Meeting the next day, the student body was astonished to learn some very unexpected news: Tripper Murphy was leaving the race for student body president, in order, he said, "to spend more time on his studies." That left Ankh-hoptet—or "Annie Hoptet," as she was called at Greenblud— running unopposed.

"It would be disrespectful to the school for me to run without my full commitment," said Tripper, as he stood in the assembly making his announcement.

"Are you certain about this?" asked Mrs. Houndstooth, as if she were afraid that Tripper was up to something.

That's because he is up to something, Falcon thought, although what it was he was up to was still not entirely clear. He looked around for Megan, to exchange glances with her, but he couldn't find her.

"Yes, Mrs. Houndstooth," said Tripper. "I have other things to focus on instead." His eyes fell on Sparkbolt, and Malcolm, and Olga, and Ankh-hoptet, who were all seated next to each other.

"Well, I'm sure everyone congratulates you on the maturity of your decision," said Mrs. Houndstooth, slowly. "And so— unless I am mistaken, that means that Miss Hoptet is the only candidate—?"

"It is so," said Ank-hoptet.

"Well, in that case," said Mrs. Houndstooth. "I think we have a new student body president. Congratulations, Miss Hoptet!"

There was a round of applause and cheers. Ankh-hoptet had managed to make a lot of friends on the women's soccer team that fall, and a win for Ankh-hoptet was seen as a win not only for her team, but for all the girls in Greenblud.

"My dynasty now begins," she said. "And so shall honor my ancestors Aakheperenre Thutmose and Maatkare Hatshepsut!"

"Awesome!" shouted Cheese.

"And Ankh-heperure Smenkh-kare as well! And Ankh-nebma-atremery-amun Ramesses!"

"Ankh ankh ankh," said Muffy, making it sound like a car horn.

"Thank you, Miss Hoptet," said Mrs. Houndstooth uncertainly.

"This is not the occasion of laughter," said Ankh-hoptet.

"Ankh ankh," said Pigpen, laughing.

"Ankh! Ankh! Ankh!" said Lemon. There was a round chorus of laughter.

"My dynasty shall not begin with tones of levity!" said Ankh-hoptet.

"Dude," said Pigpen. "Laughter's the best medicine!"

"I shall determine what is the best medicine!" shouted Ankh-hoptet.

"If I may be permitted to suggest, you highness," said Mr. Connelly, rising up out of his folding chair in the front row, where he was sitting with the rest of the faculty. "I do believe that you have chosen wisely. That by beginning your time as our ruler with a sense of lightness and mirth, that you show your justness and your wisdom." He then sat down.

A strange silence fell upon the student body. Then Ankh-hoptet said, uncertainly. "Ha-LO-oh! I— yes. I choose—laughter! The medicine that heals! Let healing thus come— to all my peoples! It is so."

There was a little applause, as the students of Greenblud High approved of Ankh-hoptet's new reign.

"Together let us wear the boots of Ugg!"

Everyone laughed at this, as if Ankh-hoptet were the funniest person any of them had ever seen.

"Dude," said Cheese. "You crack me up!"

"If you don't mind," Mrs. Houndstooth said. "I have another announcement to make, one that is considerably more difficult."

The students settled down a little, and grew silent as it became clear that Mrs. Houndstooth seemed considerably upset.

"I regret to inform you that one of our students has—withdrawn. Johnny Frankenstein returned to his family yesterday for personal reasons. I know that all of us will miss Mr. Frankenstein, who during his short time as a Greenblud student gave so much of himself. We will miss Johnny— especially his music."

There was a short moment of silence, as Falcon thought— personal reasons?

"All right then," said Mrs. Houndstooth. "I believe that is all we have for now. Let's have a good day together, shall we?"

The student body rose. Ankh-hoptet looked over at Mr. Connelly. He nodded at her.

"Thank you," said Ankh-hoptet.

"Looks to me like you're on to something," said Mr. Connelly.

"What is this that I am on upon?" asked Ankh-hoptet.

"That the best leader is the one who makes others laugh."

"Is it this I have learned?"

"People think laughter is easy," said Mr. Connelly. "But they are wrong."

Ankh-hoptet nodded. "I will henceforward devote myself to learning the language of the funny."

Mr. Connelly nodded again. "Good luck," he said.

Falcon had first period free, and after morning meeting broke up, he walked over to Megan's dorm room and knocked.

"What," said a voice, and Falcon swung open the door to find Muffy Chicago lying on her back on her bed, staring up at the ceiling.

"Oh, sorry," said Falcon. "I was just looking for—"

"She's not here," said Muffy. "Your little girlfriend. She's gone."

"She's not my—" Falcon stopped. "What do you mean, gone?"

"I mean gone. Fortunately for her. Before she found out about you and Malcolm."

"Wait, what?"

"Duh. Everybody knows about you two. How you're so much more than just roommates. Maybe that's why she vanished. To get away from you."

"Wait," said Falcon. "Vanished?"

"I haven't seen her since Sunday night," said Muffy. "She said she was going over to Johnny Frankenstein's room. Funny how they're both gone. Don't you think?"

"Did you tell anybody?" said Falcon. "Does Mrs. Houndstooth know she's gone?"

"I told my R.A.," said Muffy. "I told Judy Underhill."

Falcon thought about the last time he had seen Megan, when she'd stumbled, heartbroken, out of Jonny's room after the slime-monster attack. He felt his twin hearts begin to beat in his chest. What if that creature had come back?

"Why didn't you look out for her?" said Falcon, angrily.

"I don't know," said Muffy. "Why didn't you?"

At that moment Falcon felt a stranger looking over his shoulder. "Oh," said Merideath, from out in the hall. "It's only you."

"Did you know Megan is missing?" said Falcon.

"Lucky," said Merideath, putting her books down on Megan's bed.

"It's not funny," said Falcon. "She's in trouble!"

Merideath and Muffy both laughed.

"What's so funny?" said Falcon.

"You know who's in trouble?" Merideath said, and gave Falcon a hard look. "You."

•

Falcon rushed down the hallway to Judy Underhill's room, and he knocked on the door. At first there was no answer. But then he heard a voice. It sounded like she was moaning.

"Judy?" he said. "Are you in there? Are you all right?"

"I'm coming," she said. After a long moment, the door opened. Judy Underhill didn't look good. It looked like she'd been crying.

"Falcon Quinn," she said. "Why are you here?"

"We need to talk," said Falcon.

She looked weary, and perhaps a little suspicious. Falcon wasn't in this dorm, and so technically he was not her responsibility. But Judy just nodded to a soft chair. She sat down on a small couch next to it. Falcon was impressed; he had known that the dorm proctors had particularly good lodgings, but Judy Underhill's suite was palatial. In one corner there was even a fireplace with a mantelpiece. Above the mantel was a mirror.

"I think I know what this is about," she said.

"Do you?" said Falcon. "I kind of doubt that."

"You want to talk about James McNinch, don't you?"

Falcon opened his mouth, then closed it. This wasn't the thing that had driven him to her door, but now that he was here, he wondered. Everything, it appeared, led back to James McNinch, and his disappearance the year before.

"What do you know?" said Falcon.

"Oh, Falcon," she said. "I know everything."

"Everything?"

"I swore I wouldn't tell anyone," she said. "But now I know—you're like me."

"What do you mean?"

"Come on now," said Judy. "You don't have to pretend anymore. I figured it out last week. When I saw you and Max Parsons and Megan Crofton, out on the quad."

"You—what? What are you talking about?"

"I saw your wings come out," said Judy. "After you kissed her. I saw her disappear. She's a wind elemental. You're an angel. Max— well, actually, I don't know what Max is. I'm guessing Sasquatch, though. He's got Bigfoot written all over him."

"I—" said Falcon. "I don't know what you're talking about." He knew how unconvincing this sounded. He felt his heart pounding in his chest, and he looked around Judy's room in panic. In one corner, next to the fireplace, was a long sword.

"Oh, that," said Judy. "That's the Sword of Damocles. Have you heard of it?"

"The Sword of—"

"Damocles," said Judy. "My father gave it to me. He said I might need it some day."

"What would you need it for?"

"To kill myself with," said Judy. "If it turned out I took after my mother."

"Your mother?"

"Look," said Judy, pointing to the mirror above the fireplace. "Look at us."

"Listen, Judy," said Falcon. "I don't know what you're—"

"It's all right," said Judy. "I'm not afraid of myself any more. I used to be, but now I think it's— beautiful."

"Judy," said Falcon.

"Please," said Judy. "Just look."

Falcon sighed and stood. He walked over to the fireplace and saw himself reflected in the mirror, not as he appeared to be, but as he truly was. His wings were gathered high over his head. His halo glowed red.

Next to him, looking over his shoulder, was a hideous decaying corpse. One of its eyeballs was missing from its socket. The long hair brushed against the mortified skin.

Falcon turned swiftly to look at Judy, who, here in the room, looked like herself again. "I didn't know it was me," she said. "When I used to look in that mirror. I thought it was some horrible zombie. But slowly I figured it out. I figured it out when James came over."

"It's a Black Mirror," said Falcon. "I've seen one of these before. It shows not what you look like on the surface, but what you are, inside."

"I'm a zombie," said Judy. "You're an angel. This proves it. But I knew it before, when I saw you transform out on the quad."

"What happened to James McNinch?" said Falcon. "What was he?"

"He was a frost worm," said Judy. "Almost seven feet long, once he'd transformed. He could burrow through the snow. And he made this amazing sound. It could shatter glass. It was terrifying."

"Was he—" said Falcon. "Was he afraid of it?"

"At first. We were— we were going out that semester. It was right after I looked into the Black Mirror and saw myself for the first time. Although I didn't know it was me. But one night we looked in and we saw each other and we knew. We were standing right here."

Judy Underhill looked sad. "We learned not to be afraid, together. If it hadn't been for him, I'd never have seen myself." She turned back to the mirror. "I'd have been scared. Instead of accepting myself. For what I am. Which is someone who has power over death! Someone strong!"

"Where is he?" said Falcon. "What happened to him?"

"The thing came for him," said Judy.

"What thing?"

"The same thing that came for Johnny Frankenstein. The same thing that's coming after all of us."

"That— slime?"

"Yes," said Judy. "The slime. It hates itself. It doesn't understand what it is. So it comes in and attacks us. It comes when you're weak. That's how it got Jonny. That's how it'll get the rest of you. How many are you?"

"How many what?"

"Monsters," said Judy. "Come on, you might as well tell me. Did someone send you?"

Falcon was uncertain about telling her everything, even though she was a monster too. "We're seven in all. You're right about Megan and Max. There were nine originally: us, plus Jonny, Merideath, Sparkbolt, Destynee, Weems, and Ankh-hoptet. You're right. We were sent here to rescue you, and the others."

"What others?"

"There are five of you in all. The Academy— that's where we're from, the Academy for Monsters— wiped your brains and ran you through the Bland-a-tron, to disguise you. So the Guardians wouldn't get you. Only now you're all reverting. We have to get you out of here before you all turn back."

"Five— including James?"

"Yeah," said Falcon.

"Who are the others?"

"I don't know," said Falcon. "But time's running out. The Guardians aren't killing monsters any more. But humans are worse. They don't like it if you're different."

"You can say that again," said Judy. "So there's five in all— me, John McNinch, and the Slime—plus two more?"

"I guess," said Falcon. "Do you have any sense— who might be a monster, and who's not?"

Judy just looked sad. "Everybody seems like a monster to me," she said. "But it won't be long now. "It'll come back, the Slime, in two weeks. I know it."

"How do you know it?"

"It comes when people are all mixed up, when tensions are high. And that's Parents Weekend."

"It will come on Parents Weekend?"

Judy nodded. "What's more confusing?" she asked. "Than parents?"

10.

Parents' Weekend

Autumn came early to New Hampshire. Long before
Halloween arrived, the maples turned a screaming crimson, then
slowly grew more bare as the winds of winter blew in. By the final
days of October, all the leaves were on the ground, and raked into
piles by the groundskeepers at Greenblud.

On the Friday night before the parents arrived, Falcon sat in his
room, looking through his window at the main quad, where Cheese
and Pigpen and a few of the others were jumping into the piles of
leaves. The sounds of their laughter, the crunch and rustle of the
leaves beneath them as they landed in the piles, reached his ears. It
was an abnormally warm day in Indian summer, but the sun shone
down at an oblique angle, casting long shadows on the quad even in
mid-afternoon.

He watched as the wind lifted the piles of orange leaves and
spun them around in tiny cyclones. As the leaves were caught up in
the gust, you could see the wind move from one side of the quad to
another. The last few leaves still in the trees fell to earth, drifting
downward in the same direction as the slanting yellow light.

Megan had never come back after blinking out that night. He kept expecting her to reappear, but to no avail. Mrs. Houndstooth had announced her departure at a morning meeting in the same disinterested tone that she'd used when she'd told everyone about Johnny. No one seemed too worried, though; Megan, like Jonny, was a new student, and apparently people left Greenblud all the time, sometimes because they'd broken the rules, other times because their grades weren't good enough. No one seemed to be concerned that people weren't just leaving— they were disappearing. No one, that is, except for the monsters with whom he'd come here, and even they seemed, at times, to be settling into their new community, acting like they belonged to this place, that they were part of it, rather than monsters sent here in disguise in order to perform an urgent mission. Even now, as he looked out the window, he could see Weems and Destynee, sitting on a bench watching Cheese and Pigpen jumping into leaves. Ankh-hoptet was standing not far away, surrounded by the girls on the soccer team. Another cyclone of leaves blew across the quad, and Falcon felt his face growing warm. His shoulder blades ached where his wings would be.

Weems threw back his head and laughed, and Destynee looked at him with an amused, happy expression. He couldn't believe his own eyes: Weems, who never laughed at anything, and Destynee, who'd only weeks ago watched as Johnny Frankenstein was absorbed into the pulsing mass of the Slime? He gritted his teeth, reached forward and picked up a book from his desk and threw it against the wall.

"What's wrong with all of you!" he shouted, as he threw the book. But at that moment Falcon was aware of another presence in his room. Max reached up and with one hand caught the volume.

"Dude," he said.

Pearl was right behind him. "My friend," she said. "It is disheartening to see you in this state!"

Falcon glowered at them both for a moment, then he felt the black cloud upon him lift a little bit. It still amused him to see Pearl and Max camouflaged as humans, especially Pearl, whom he could never quite look upon without seeing her in her Chupakabra form—a small flying spright with a long poisonous stinger.

"Hey," he said.

"Hey yourself," said Max, looking at the book he had caught. It was the Collected Works of Shakespeare. "We wanted to know if you wanted to go bouncing, man."

"Oh Max," said Falcon. "I don't think I can bounce."

"I for one am unfamiliar with this art," said Pearl. "But I have pledged my friendship to Max! And so! I shall bounce! With honor and courage I shall see it done!"

"Bouncing doesn't take any courage," said Max. "It's just bouncing."

"I don't know," said Falcon. "Sometimes I think being happy takes a lot of courage."

"My friend!" said Pearl. "It pains me to find you in this state! And yet none could fault you for your sadness! We have suffered our losses! Megan Crofton, the Wind Elemental— invisible upon the breeze itself! And Señor Frankenstein, our friend!—who without warning, has—has gone his separate ways!"

"I just don't get it," said Falcon, looking out the window. "Look at them all! How can everybody be so happy?"

"Hey man," said Max. "Being happy's hard. Being all sad about everything, that's the easy thing. Being happy, when you know how hard everything is? Only a total genius can do that."

"Looks like a lot of geniuses out there," said Falcon. His shoulders still ached where his wings should be.

"My friend," said Pearl, sitting down on his bed. "I would not tell you to be not sad, for sometimes there is greater wisdom in sadness than in joy."

"No way," said Max. "What are you talking about? I tell ya man, the main thing is bouncing, dude! We just gotta! Then you'll feel—"

"Senor Max!" said Pearl sternly. "No one can find their joy by being told to do so! The heart follows its own path! No brave soul finds its courage without sorrow."

"I wish we had never come here," said Falcon. "I wish we were back on Monster Island."

"She'd have disappeared there, too, man," said Max. Falcon looked at him harshly. "Meggers. She's a wind elemental, dude. That's what she is. She's supposed to vanish. Become the wind. That's like her job."

"I just miss her," said Falcon. "It's not fair. I finally kiss my girlfriend, and she turns invisible."

"Yeah, but you had that moment, right?" said Max. "That night? She totally loved you. She'll always love you, man."

"How do I know that?" said Falcon. "What does that even mean?"

"My friend," said Pearl. She went to the window and threw up the sash. The curtains billowed into the room. "She is here with you now."

Papers on Falcons desk blew onto the floor. The curtains hovered and fluttered like ghosts.

"Megan our friend! We salute your courage, in becoming your self at last!"

Falcon didn't look convinced. "How do we even know this is her?" he said.

"Because—" said Max. "She's like— uh—"

"We do not know this," said Pearl. "It is true. But one can believe. This is what it means to have faith. To believe in the unseen."

"I'm tired of believing in the unseen!" shouted Falcon. "Just once I'd like to believe in something I could touch."

There was a pause as Pearl and Max took this in. Tears quavered on Falcon's eyelashes. Then he felt Pearl's hand on his shoulder. "We shall always stand by you, Falcon Quinn," she said. "It is in your friends that you must trust."

"Yeah," said Max, putting his hand on Falcon's other shoulder. "You'll always have us."

"Ah, there you are!" said a voice, and they looked to the door to see Judy Underhill looking at them. Falcon had let the others know that Judy was one of the missing monsters, that there were only two left yet to find.

"My undead friend!" said Pearl. "It is an honor to have been the object of your search!"

"Your parents are here," said Judy. "They're looking for you."

"Wait, what?" said Max. "I haven't seen my parents since—"

"They are here. They've been run through the Bland-a-tron. They look just like humans."

"Wait," said Max. "My parents were monsters? No way."

"Leprachauns, I think," said Judy. "Seriously, they didn't tell you this? They're kind of adorable."

"Whoa whoa whoa," said Max. "I'm a Sasquatch, dude. I'm six feet six inches tall, maybe three hundred pounds wet out of the shower? And my parents are—"

"Tiny little people," said Judy. "Go on and meet them. They're out on the quad." She looked at Pearl. "Yours too."

"My parents have come to this Neuvo Hampshire? From Peru they have come?"

"Yeah," said Judy. "Most of the parents are here. They had to Bland-a-rize them all so they look like humans, but they're here. They want to see you."

"My father! Don Carlo de Chupakabro Borges Villasquez! And my mother Sophia los Muerta! Come! We shall welcome them with honor!"

"You go ahead," said Falcon. "I'll be down."

"My friend," said Pearl. "You must not dishonor me by refusing to meet my mother and my father, whom I respect above all others! They are—Los Chupakabras! The famous goatsuckers of Peru!"

"I said I'll be down," said Falcon.

"Promise," said Max.

"I promise," said Falcon.

He and Pearl hugged their friend, then took their leave. Judy nodded at him, then followed the others outside. Falcon stood in the window and looked out on the quad. Slowly the curtains fell as the wind died down. Whatever had been in the room before was gone now.

Falcon felt his two hearts beating hard. It's not Megan that I'm missing now, he thought. It's my parents.

He looked out on the green quad, now slowly filling with visitors, mothers and fathers arriving in ones and twos. There was Gunk with his father, a man with a plaid shirt and an enormous beer belly. There was Malcolm with his grandmother, a woman with a beehive hairdo and a laugh so loud he could hear it from up here. There was Olga, surrounded by two people who looked so much like her it would almost have been amusing, were it not for the grave and proud expressions on their faces. Everyone had a mother or a father, he thought. People that they loved or hated. People with whom they had everything, or nothing, in common. Mothers and fathers, each in their own awkward, sometimes inarticulate way, trying to watch over their sons and daughters. Everyone had someone, Falcon thought.

Except me.

"Excuse me," said a voice. Falcon turned to see an odd looking man wearing a long white coat. There were stains and burn marks on it. The man's head was bald on top, but with long frizzy hair on the sides. He wore a pair of glasses that were so thick they made his eyes look gigantic. "I'm looking for Falcon Quinn. Might you be himself?"

"I'm Falcon," he said. "Who are you?"

"Ah, he was right. You are just as he described you!" The man looked enraptured.

"Who?"

"Mr. Lyons his name was, although I understand, yes? He has other names? Indeed. He sent me to find you. That you are the one who can help me find my boy."

"Your boy?" said Falcon.

"Yes," said the man. "His name is Jonny. For so long I have sought him."

Falcon swallowed. "You're looking for—"

The man's eyes teared up. "My dear, dear boy," he said. "He is all I live for. My own son, whom I thought I had lost forever. Jonny—? Jonny Frankenstein?"

•

There was a football game at noon, Greenblud against the East
Central Normal School, which the "Greyskins" of Normal beat the
Greenblud Greenies by a score of 58-3, a considerable
embarrassment for Mr. Wilson, the coach, not to mention the teams
quarterback, Lemon, who was sacked an astonishing eleven times,
and Gunk, the wide receiver, who fumbled over a dozen passes, at
least four of which led to turnovers and an eventual touchdown by
the Greyskins. About the only member of the Greenies who was not
embarrassed by the performance was Sparkbolt, who scored the
teams one and only field goal.

It was Halloween, and the Greenblud students, and many of
their parents, were wearing costumes. For the hidden monsters from
the Academy, this provided a strange opportunity— to walk around
in the world wearing their own actual identities as a mask.
Merideath was dressed up like a vampire, Ankh-hoptet like a
Princess of Ancient Egypt. But then other Greenblud students were
disguised as well. Quacky was dressed up like a zombie; Malcolm,
Falcon's roommate, was a lumberjack.

Falcon watched the game from the bleachers with Johnny's
father, whom he had told only that his son had left the school several
weeks past, and that they'd all been told the boy had gone back to
his home. "His mothers, I suppose," Dr. Frankenstein said, with an
air of exhaustion.

"I didn't know Jonny had a mother," said Falcon, without thinking.

On the field before them, there was another interception by the Greyskins, and everyone in the stands groaned as the visiting team ran eighty yards for yet another touchdown.

"Now I wonder what you mean by that, yes I do," said Dr. Frankenstein.

"Nothing," said Falcon. "He just never said anything about her."

"I see. But then did he ever say anything about me I suspect he did not?"

"Not much," said Falcon.

"Ah, not much, yes, I see." Dr. Frankenstein got a handkerchief out of his pocket and mopped his forehead with it. There were big burn marks in the handkerchief. "You have known Jonny for a long time I suspect, yes. I suspect you know more of him than you can say."

"I haven't known him all that long," said Falcon.

"It's just that my research has kept me so busy," said Dr. Frankenstein, pulling his glasses off and rubbing them with the hem of his long lab coat. "There are times when I have lost all track of things. Johnny, and his mother of course. One day I realized her things had been gone from the house for some time. How long had this been? Months? I don't know. I should have had more care, I should have, I should have. You see my research has been all wrong, all wrong the whole time. I have spent my life studying the wrong things, can you understand? I suspect not."

A horn blew and the game ended, and the Greenblud Greenies slunk off of the field. The spectators up in the stands wasted no time in taking their leave. It seemed as if only seconds after the game had ended, it was just down to Falcon and Jonny's father and a few stragglers. The players from Central Normal climbed on board a big yellow school bus.

Destynee and Weems approached them. "Hi Falcon," said Destynee. She and Weems were holding hands. Destynee was dressed up like a vampire; Weems was wearing a Batman mask.

"Hey," said Falcon. "This is Dr. Frankenstein. Jonny's father."

"What?" said Destynee. She looked confused. "But I thought he didn't have a—"

"Oh but he did, and that father was me," said Dr. Frankenstein. "Although, hm, I suspect I was not a father in the sense that you might mean, but I was his father all the same." He looked at Destynee and Weems. "You were his friends? I see you were. You knew him then."

"We did," said Weems. "He was good to us. We always thought he was so very crunchy sweet."

"All of you knew him then," said Dr. Frankenstein. He ran his hand over his bald crown. "You knew him, and I did not. And now it is too late, too late! I suspect I will never know him now."

"I loved Jonny," said Destynee. Weems looked at her restlessly. "I loved him so much!"

"I—" Dr. Frankenstein got out his handkerchief again. "I will never have that chance, I suspect, I will not. Tell me—" He looked around nervously. "Were you with him at the end, were you?"

"The end," said Weems, "we wonder what it means by that exactly."

"Yeah," said Falcon. "We just heard one morning that he had…"

"Oh, it is my fault," said Dr. Frankenstein. "It is all my fault!"

"What's your fault?" said Destynee. "What do you mean?"

"The design," said the doctor, shaking his head. "I discovered it later. Such a simple mistake, anyone could have made it?"

"What design does it mean, we wonder," said Weems. "It is very mysterious."

"The design of my boy!" shouted the doctor. "He was doomed from the start! The centrifuge was off center. Of course he dissolved, it was inevitable, because of my own stupidity! I was— ashamed!" Tears quavered in his eyes. "I fled from him. My own son! Because I was— afraid. That he would blame me."

"Blame you for what?" said Destynee.

The doctor shook his head. "For the mistake in the design. And then, after, for the mistake I made when I fled. Now it is too late. Too late! He is not with the mother, is he? No, he is not. You must all have been with him when it happened. You are trying to protect him, but you do not need to keep this secret. Not from me. Not from the one who is to blame."

"Blame bad," said a voice, and they all looked up to see Sparkbolt standing there in his football uniform, holding his helmet in one hand.

"Oh my goodness, look at you," said the doctor, his face brightening suddenly. "Why— you're one of my children!"

"Rrar," said Sparkbolt.

"Of course!" shouted the doctor. "You're Sparkbolt, aren't you! Sparkboltt!" The doctor jumped to his feet. "You're alive! Alive!" The man threw his arms around Sparkbolt.

"Rrar!" said Sparkbolt. "Man strange."

"Wait," said Falcon. "You're saying— you made Sparkbolt too?"

"Falcon," said Destynee. "Ix-nay on the upid-say,"

"Come come come," said the doctor. "I think we may all speak freely."

"Freedom bad," said Sparkbolt.

"No, freedom good," said the doctor. "Don't you see? It's me, son. I'm your father."

Sparkbolt looked at the doctor uncertainly, and as he did a series of emotions coursed across his face: confusion, anger, fear, and then, finally, something that looked at lot like love. "Poppy?" said Sparkbolt. "Sparkbolt— Poppy?"

"Yes," said Dr. Frankenstein. "It's me. I've found you at last. And I'm never going to leave you again. I'm going to take care of you."

"Wait," said Falcon. He realized he seemed to be saying 'wait' a lot. "So Sparkbolt and Jonny are— brothers?"

"Jonny," said Sparkbolt, and his eyes filled with tears. "Brother. Dead."

"Dead you say?" the doctor said. "Were you there, son? When he dissolved?"

"No, it was me and Destynee and Megan," said Falcon. "He— went all to pieces."

"Yes, yes, I know!" shouted the doctor. "Because of the design. It was bound to happen. That's why I have been looking for him, everywhere. I wanted to fix him before the malfunction."

"Sparkbolt— broken?" said Sparkbolt. "Sparkbolt too?"

"No," said the doctor. "I saw what I'd done. I fixed it when I made you. Jonny was the rough draft, don't you see. When I made you I'd perfected the method."

"Rrar," said Sparkbolt, smiling grimly. "Perfected."

"If only we had the pieces," said the doctor. "I could correct my mistake. Restore him! That's what I wanted. But I'm too late, I suspect. Oh, all too late!" The doctor looked around uncertainly. "You don't have the pieces do you? Did you save them?"

"He got eaten by a gigantic Slime thing," said Destynee. "It appeared out of nowhere and sucked up the pieces and then it disappeared."

"A Slime monster!" said the doctor, clapping his hands together. "Fantastic!" He jumped into the air. "Oh, finally some good news!"

"It reacts very strangely," said Weems.

"Don't you see, don't you see," said Dr. Frankenstein. "The pieces will be kept fresh in the slime, just like they'd been saved in plastic wrap! All we have to do is find that Slime, extract the pieces of Jonny, and we can put him together again, good as new! Better than new, in fact! For now I know how to keep him from falling apart!" He looked at Destynee suspiciously. "Were you the one who bit him?" he said.

"I beg your pardon," said Destynee.

"You're the vampire, I presume," said the doctor. He looked at Weems. "You're a ghoul, that's clear."

"I'm not a vampire," said Destynee. "I'm an enchanted giant slug."

"Wait," said Falcon, again. "How do you know what we all are? We're disguised as humans. No one's supposed to be able to tell what we are."

"I have weird-dar," said the doctor. "I can see a monster just like that," and he snapped his fingers. A small spark of flame came from his fingertips.

"I did not bite him," said Destynee. "Although——"

"It was Merideath," said Weems. "It was the one who trapped him, on Monster Island."

"Wait," said the doctor, looking at Falcon. "I'm having some—
-" He got his singed handkerchief out again. "What are you, son?
For some reason I can't—"

"I'm an angel," said Falcon.

"Of course," said the doctor. "An angel." Then he looked
uncertain. "But then— an angel isn't exactly a monster, is it?
You're something different, yes I suspect you are. No wonder Jonny
was drawn to you. He would have seen something of himself. The
outcast. The black sheep. The red-headed stepchild."

"Him friend," said Sparkbolt. "Falcon good."

"Well of course," said the doctor. "He is an angel, isn't he?" He
looked at Sparkbolt. "You know I can fix your voice functions, if
you like. The software you're running is completely out of date."

"Software bad," said Sparkbolt.

"It can help us then," said Weems, excitedly. "It can help."

"Well of course I can —"

"No, no, it listens," said Weems. "It has the weird-dar. It can
help us find the hidden ones."

"Hidden?" said Dr. Frankenstein.

"Yes, hidden!" said Weems. "It can help us with the mission."

"We were sent here by the Academy," said Falcon. "They ran us
through a Bland-a-tron so we could spy on the students here. There
are five hidden monsters here we have to find, before they revert
back to their monster forms and cause havoc. We already know
about three of them— a boy named McNinch who got absorbed by
the Slime last year. And a girl named Judy Underhill, she's a

zombie. And the Slime itself, of course, although we don't know where it lives.'

"Ah," said the doctor. "So there are two more monsters to find. Plus the Slime. Yes. I can help. It is good we found each other. I can help you, and you can help me. I can find your missing monsters, I suspect, and yes, then we can get Jonny's pieces out of the Slime, and I can reassemble my boy. And tell him I love him! I will tell all my sons that I love them. Just like I love you, Sparkbolt! My most perfect creation!"

"Perfect," said Sparkbolt.

"So it's all settled then," said Falcon.

"Uh-oh," said Destynee.

"Wait," said Falcon. "What's uh-oh?"

There was a rumbling sound. Destynee pointed to a sewer grate that stood next to the grandstand. The ground shook. All at once a molten green slime bubbled out of the sewer, gathered shape on the grounds, and then ascended the steps up into the bleachers.

"It stands back!" shouted Weems. "It will not attack the Beloved!"

But the Slime just vibrated and made a deep sound like hawgh-hawgh-hawgh. It bubbled and gurgled. There were pieces of all sorts of glop in it. For a moment, surfacing out of its depths, was the head of Jonny Frankenstein.

"My— my boy!" shouted the doctor.

But then the Slime oozed forward and consumed the doctor. There was a hissing sound, and Dr. Frankenstein's eyes turned white, like hard boiled eggs. Then he was sucked entirely into the vibrating, gelatinous mass. The Slime made that sound again, hawgh-hawgh-hawgh, and then gurgled back down the stairs and disappeared into the sewer. With a final clank it put the grate back on top of the sewer. The ground shook once, twice, and then everything fell silent again.

The four friends stood in the empty grandstand looking at the place where the Slime had been.

Weems pointed into the sewer. "We must go down there."

Destynee, still wearing her vampire costume, wrinkled her nose. "Ew," she said. "Gross."

"Poppy?" said Sparkbolt. His voice caught. "Poppy?"

11.

The Horn of Vrzøzyz

The concert for the parents was being held in a space called the Cafetoriasium, a multi-purpose room that had originally been a cafeteria, then was refitted to serve part time as an auditorium,

making it the Cafetorium, and then refitted again to also serve as a
gymnasium, giving it its current unpronounceable name. There
were, in fact, plans currently under review to add some laboratory
space for AP chemistry to the room, making it the
Cafetoriasiumbratory. In the time to come here were lots of
possibilities possible. For now, students and their families sat on
hundreds of folding chairs fanning out before the makeshift stage.
At five to seven, the room was nearly full. Almost everyone in the
audience was wearing a Halloween costume.

"Dude," said Max, peeking from behind a curtain. He was
dressed up like a Sasquatch, which in Max's case, wasn't hard. Two
Little People waved at him, and he smiled. "Whoa," he said. "It's
my maw and paw! They made them little!"

"Max," said Malcolm. He was wearing his lumberjack duds—a
plaid shirt and big boots. "Stop peeking."

"Okay, okay," said Max. He looked at his watch. "Where's
Sparkbolt? We're on in five minutes!"

"He shall be cursed, for all time," said Ankh-hoptet. On her
head was the funerary mask of a pharaoh. "His bowels shall be
cremated and preserved in an urn of poison. Scented with cinnamon
and arsenic his remains shall be!"

Malcolm laughed. "You're so funny," he said. He glanced at
the music. "So is everybody ready? We open with 'Peace Like a
River.' Then it's on to 'Til There Was You.'"

"Rrar," said a voice, and Sparkbolt arrived, all out of breath.

"Dude," said Max. "Where have you been? We were all freaking out!"

"Game," said Sparkbolt. "Football bad."

"Indeed," said Ankh-hoptet. "Your team bears the curse. You must have broken the sacred seal upon the tomb of the undead!"

"No seal," said Sparkbolt. "Need love."

Malcolm looked at Sparkbolt curiously. "Love?" he said. "You think the Greenies would have won that game today if they'd had more love?"

Sparkbolt nodded, and, to Malcolm's amazement, tears quivered in the young man's eyes. "Everybody need love," said Sparkbolt.

Malcolm shook his head. "Sparky, you are a-may-zing."

"Rrrar." said the Frankenstein. "Ruff." He sniffed.

"Dude," said Max. "Are you okay? You seem kind of wonkaly."

"Sparkbolt good," said Sparkbolt. "Love strong."

"Everybody ready?" said Malcolm. "Here we go."

Mrs. Houndstooth stepped up to the microphone. "Good evening students, and welcome parents. It is my pleasure to introduce to you at this time, our singing quartet, the Bludstones!"

The audience applauded, and out came the foursome: Malcolm, Sparkbolt, Ankh-hoptet, and Max. Spark bolt gave them the opening note. "Rrrrer," he sang.

And then they all began to sing.

Falcon, arriving late, sat down in a chair at the back the auditorium, and listened to the beautiful voices of his friends. "I've got peace like a river," they sang. "I've got peace like a river in my soul." Their voices wrapped around each other so perfectly it was almost impossible to know which voice belonged to which monster.

Of course they're not all monsters, Falcon thought. Malcolm's a human being. His hearts ached as he thought about the way Malcolm had been bullied and hurt earlier in the semester. Falcon felt sad as he realized, and not for the first time, that you didn't have to be a monster to be made to feel like you were less than something human. Some day, Falcon thought, some day no one is going to suffer any more. He wondered what he could do to help bring that world about. It seemed impossible, that anyone could push back against all the meanness and loss people carried around.

He looked up at the ceiling as he listened to the voices. Up there was a metallic bridge, from which the stage lights were suspended. As he stared, Falcon saw something move for a single second. His hearts beat even faster now.

Someone was up there on the lighting bridge, suspended directly over the place where the Bludstones were singing.

There was a small door in the wall at the end of the bridge, and as Falcon watched, he saw another figure, clothed all in black, gently pass through it.

This didn't make any sense, Falcon thought. What were they doing?

"I've got love like an ocean," the Bludstones sang. "I've got love like an ocean in my soul."

Falcon felt another twinge in his hearts, and thought, well, great for you. Here he was, sitting in the Cafetoriasium, with all the mommies and daddies of Greenblud. Max's tiny parents sat in the front row, swinging their legs back and forth from their folding chairs. Ankh-hoptet's daddy, a mummy, watched gravely. All around him were the students of this community and their parents, tall and short, black and white, old and young. Even Sparkbolt had a father, it seemed. Everyone has someone, Falcon thought. Except for me. He thought about Vega and the Crow, whom he'd seen back in that stupid barn with Mr. Swishtail. They'd acted as if he were a person of no consequence.

Gunk, dressed all in black, opened a door off to one side of the Cafetoriasium, and Falcon now knew that it was Gunk whom he had seen up on the light bridge, handing something to somebody else, somebody who was still up there, perched just above the place where the Bludstones were singing. Gunk headed toward the audience, then stopped. He raised one hand to his neck as if he was choking. He looked around with an expression Falcon had never seen on his face before— a face of panic. Then he turned around, swiftly, and headed for an exit at the back of the room.

"I've got joy like a fountain," the Bludstones sang. "I've got joy like a fountain in my soul."

That's weird, Falcon thought. Where's he going?

•

"This is so gross," said Destynee, as she walked through the sewer.

"I find something about it pleasingly macabre," said Weems. "I can just imagine small creatures finding their way in here, and being trapped. Forever!" He smiled happily.

"You're twisted," said Destynee.

"Yes," said Weems, clasping his small white hands together. "Yes!"

"What are we going to do if we find... if we find this slime?" said Desytnee. "It didn't look like it was the kind of slime you could reason with exactly."

"It is our mission," said Weems. "We shall do as we have been asked. And then—Oh how I hope— we may leave this accursed place. This place of doom."

"Do you mean this sewer?" said Destynee. "Or high school in general."

There was a small trickle of effluvium at the bottom of the large culvert. The pipe was so large that they could almost stand upright. They had to be careful, though, not to let their shoes fall into the greywater.

"I mean this place where we must conceal ourselves," said Weems. "Where we cannot be our true selves."

"I kind of like being human," said Destynee. "It's better than being a Giant Enchanted Slug."

Weems, who was just ahead of Destynee in the sewer, stopped and looked back at her beseechingly. "You must not say this about yourself. Whatever you are, is beautiful and crunchy."

"Well, you like being a ghoul," said Destynee. "It is easy for you to say."

"It is not easy for me to say!" shouted Weems. "It is torture!"

"What is torture!"

Weems looked down at the trickling stream of goop. "Being with one who does not see herself."

"I see myself pretty clear," said Destynee sadly. "I see a girl who got to look normal for a month or two, out of her whole life. A girl who pretty soon has to go back to being a Giant Enchanted Slug. It's gross, Weems. I don't like it."

"Why can you not see yourself as I see you?" said Weems, and his voice caught. "There is beauty in you. It shines out from within. Can you not see it?"

"You're insane."

"Destynee," said Weems, his voice almost a sob. "I wish that you could see through my eyes. And know that you are loved."

"Ugh," said Destynee. "Please."

"There is beauty in all things," said Weems. "There is beauty in the clam. There is beauty, even in the sneezing toucan! Why should there be no beauty in ourselves, we who feel the injustice of the world, we who feel so deeply, because of our difference?"

"I know I'm a good person," said Destynee. "That's not the point. I just don't like being a slug."

"We can choose all things," said Weems. "Except our selves. These come to us as a gift from the Watcher."

Destynee screamed. One of her feet had fallen into the stream of gunk. "Are you all right?" said Weems, coming over to her, concerned. "Let me help you!"

"I don't need any help!" shouted Destynee. Her voice echoed in the sewer. "I just want you to—-" But at this moment they heard another voice coming from just ahead. It was the sound of something gurgling. It sounded sad.

"Quick," said Weems. "The slime!" He took her hand and they rushed toward the source of the sound. Ahead of them, light fell from an overhead grate and into a large square chamber. Sewer pipes from six different directions converged here, and the glop that they contained spilled from their rim and into a central tank. Sitting on the edge of the tank, like someone sitting by the banks of a stream, looking at her own reflection, was a Giant Slug.

"Whoa," said Destynee. "That's not slime!"

"No," said Weems, his eyes wide. "It is not."

"Oh, waaah, waaah, waah," wept the Slug.

"She's crying," said Weems.

"Well, why wouldn't she?"

"She weeps, " said Weems. "Because she cannot see herself!"

"Hey," said Destynee, drawing nearer to the Giant Enchanted Slug. "It's okay. It's not so bad. Really."

"Yes, exactly," said Weems. "It is a gift!"

"Go away," said the slug. It was a voice that Destynee recognized. "Leave me alone."

"You're with friends," said Destynee. "You're like me."

"That's what I hate!" said the slug. "That's why I'm crying!"

The slug vibrated for a moment and its slimy, glisteny skin shuddered. There was a flash of light, and then the slug morphed before their eyes into a thin girl with black hair and lustrous eyes.

"Muffy?" said Destynee. "Muffy Chicago?"

"Go ahead," said Muffy. "Go ahead and laugh. It's what I'd do."

"Of course we won't laugh," said Destynee. "I told you, you're like me. I'm a giant slug too."

"You are… beautiful!" said Weems, his eyes wide.

"What are you doing down here?" said Destynee. "Why are you in the sewer?"

"It's the only place I can find where no one has to look at me. When I change. And see what I am!"

"When did the change begin?" said Weems. "Has the slugfulness been part of you for— a long time?"

"Just this fall," said Slug-muffy. "It's when I get all excited. This feeling comes over me and I—" She shuddered and again she transformed into her giant slug form. Even down here in the darkness of the sewer, her moist, rubbery skin shimmered.

"There's nothing wrong with what you are!" said Destynee. "You have to make peace with it." Weems looked at her uncertainly. "What?" she said.

"You are speaking the words which we were speaking to you," said Weems.

Muffy looked at Weems like he was slightly insane. "What's he talking about?" she said. "Is he a disgusting slug too?"

"No, he's a ghoul." When Muffy's face failed to show understanding, Destynee added, "He finds little dead animals and roasts them over a fire and eats them."

"Seriously?" said Muffy. "Ugh. I can't even."

"There are a lot of us here. Monsters, in disguise. We were sent here to find five monsters who were in hiding. You have a lot of friends. There's a mummy, a Sasquatch, a Chupakabra—"

"A what?" said Muffy.

"La Chupakabra," said Weems. "It is the famous goatsucker of Peru."

"We're all in disguise," said Destynee. "We're trying to rescue you."

"That's what I want, is a disguise," said Muffy. Her skin rippled, and again she transformed back into human form. "So I never have to look at myself again!"

"But it should accept itself!" said Weems. "Accept the beauty and wonderment!"

"Next time I change," said Muffy. "I'm salting myself."

"I used to think that," said Destynee. "Now I think I was wrong."

Weems just looked at Destynee, his eyes round.

"Look, I'm sorry I was a bitch," said Muffy. "But being a gigantic slug, it brings me down."

"It's okay," said Destynee. "Lots of people are mean when they aren't happy with themselves."

"Let it apologize!" said Weems. "It has fences to mend!"

"No she doesn't," said Destynee. "Just accept yourself. You're an enchanted giant slug. There are worse things, believe me."

Muffy looked up at Destynee, the tears shining in her eyes. "What's worse than being an enchanted giant slug? Tell me one thing!"

"Why, lots of things," said Destynee. "Like, uh—-"

But at that moment there was a sudden gurgling and a sound like hawgh hawgh hawgh, and the tremendous vibrating Slime oozed out of one of the sewer pipes. It had grown larger now. It swelled in the small room, glowing and pulsing, and then in a single motion it extended one of its protoplasmic arms around Muffy Chicago. "Wait!" shouted Muffy. "Stop!"

But in another instant she was gone, absorbed into the oozing slime. The monster pulsed and swirled and once more it said, "Hawgh hawgh hawgh." And then it oozed into one of the other sewer pipes and was gone.

"The Beloved!" Weems shouted. "The Beloved!"

"I'm fine," said Destynee.

Weems seemed surprised that Destynee was still there. "We didn't mean you," he said.

•

It was twilight on the Greenblud campus as Falcon stepped out of the Cafetoriasium and onto the quad. Long shadows from the old academic buildings fell across the lawn. Falcon stood still for a moment, scanning the campus for signs of life. Then he saw Gunk, hurrying past the ivy-covered Chemistry building. Gunk cast a look over his shoulder and made eye contact with Falcon. In that moment, Falcon saw on the boys' face an expression of absolute terror.

Gunk turned his head and ran.

"Hey," Falcon shouted. "Gunk! What are you doing?"

But Gunk didn't come back.

Falcon ran after him, but as he ran, he felt his wings pushing against his shoulder blades. His dark eye began to burn in its socket. I've got to calm down, he thought. I ought to just stop and catch my breath.

But instead of this he kept on running, and his eye grew hotter.

He reached the far side of the Chemistry building and looked around for Gunk, but he didn't see anybody. The area behind the old lab— known as Icicle Hall— was surrounded with small twisted trees. Their limbs reached down toward Falcon. Most of their leaves had fallen, and gathered in piles of brown and yellow at Falcon's feet.

A small path led from Icicle Hall and into a dark forest.

For a moment, Falcon stood at the edge of the woods. He felt his hearts pounding in his chest. His dark eye burned even hotter. You should go back and get help, he thought. Don't do this alone.

Then he thought of the Cafetoriasium, filled with all those mommies and daddies, looking lovingly at their sons and daughters, everyone wearing a costume that they could simply take off at the end of the day, if they so chose. And he stepped forward onto the dark path. I'll always be alone, he thought.

•

Tripper Murphy stood on the bridge above the stage where the Bludstones were singing with the bucket full of horse manure. "I've got joy like a river," Sparkbolt sang, and just the sound of the boy's voice filled him with rage. He was half tempted to tip the bucket right at that moment, but then he took a breath. Wait, he thought. Wait for Malcolm.

Taking a breath was a mixed blessing, as it turned out, for the bucket of manure he and Gunk had gathered from the barn at the edge of the Greenblud campus filled his nostrils with a very unpleasant smell indeed. Plus there was that horse, Swishtail, that stood there the whole time, watching, and who acted as if taking its poop and putting it in a bucket was the same as stealing. Tripper bit down on the inside of his mouth to keep himself from gagging. He counted Presidents backwards in his head until he stopped feeling nauseated. Obama, Bush, Clinton, Bush, Reagan, Carter, Ford,

Nixon…. By the time he got to Nixon he was calm again. He looked at the stage below him. The Bludstones were finishing up their song, their hands in the air, big smiles on their faces. The audience began to applaud wildly.

"And now," said Ank-hoptet. "We shall feature the voice of the most loyal of my subjects, Malcolm Flynn."

Max smiled broadly. "Dude," he said. "Being class President totally went to her head!"

"I am the queen of everything!" Ank-hoptet snapped. The audience laughed. Ank-hoptet looked uncertain, then smiled.

"What did I say?" said Max. The audience laughed some more.

"My subjects shall all bow before my magnificence," said Ank-hoptet. She raised her hands. In her funerary mask, she did indeed look impressive.

Max and Malcolm and Sparkbolt smiled, and then they all bowed. The audience laughed some more, and Ank-hoptet looked pleased.

Then Malcolm stepped forward. "This song is from the musical 'Oliver!' It's called 'Where is Love?'"

The audience quieted down, and then Malcolm began to sing. At first the other Bludstones were silent and listened as the small young lumberjack sang a capella. Then they began to hum softly behind him. The voices were beautiful. Something about the way Malcolm sang captured the attention of his audience completely. Perhaps it was just that he had a beautiful singing voice. On the other hand, what with the traces of his not-quite-healed black eye

still visible on his face, it might be that the song Malcolm was
singing cut more deeply than anyone had expected.

"Will I ever know?" he sang. "The sweet hello, that I've been
dreaming of?"

That's it, Tripper thought. Now you're going down.

He picked up the bucket of manure and moved down the bridge
above the stage so that he was positioned exactly over the place
where Malcolm stood. The wafting smell from the bucket hit him
again, and Tripper felt tears stinging in his eyes.

"Where is love?" sang Malcolm. "Where is love??"

For a moment, Tripper thought of his own parents. Of all the
kids in his own group of friends, he was the only one whose parents
had not come this weekend. He told himself it didn't matter, but
then he remembered the conversation he'd had with his father on the
phone, after he'd told the old man that he hadn't been chosen as
class president, that he'd decided to step down rather than lose the
election.

When I was a Greenblud student, the old man had said. I was
president my junior and senior years. I was the unanimous choice!

Yeah, well, I'm not you, Dad, Tripper had said.

Yes, said his father, his disappointment dripping from his voice.
That is abundantly clear.

He lifted the bucket of manure and prepared to pour. A wicked
smiled flickered across his lips, and his eyes shone. I'll tell you
where love is, Tripper thought.

"My friend," said a voice.

Tripper looked down toward the end of the light bridge. A figure stood there in shadow. "No one's allowed up here," he said.

"Indeed," said the voice. "It was this itself that made me consider. What is Senor Murphy doing, from this high perch. And what might his intentions be, with the bucket of poop he holds thus in his hand?"

The figure stepped forward, and Tripper now saw that it was that new girl, Pearl.

"Get lost," Tripper said. "No freshmen are allowed up here."

"Ah," said Pearl. "But I am not a freshman."

"Yeah?" said Tripper Murphy. "What are you then?"

The girl stepped toward him, and he now saw that she held a sword in one hand, the Sword of Damocles he had once seen in the room of the Mossback proctor, Judy Underhill. "I am La Chupakabra," she said. "The famous goatsucker of Peru!"

•

Weems and Destynee walked forward in the dark. The waste water on the bottom of the culvert was not much more than a trickle in this culvert. In the distance they could see what looked like another square chamber. Dim light filtered down from a grate.

"Are we following the correct path?" said Weems. "It is not clear."

"Hmph," said Destynee.

"It is saying Hmph?" said Weems. "Hmph is the response it gives us here in the hour of need?"

"I'm not talking to you," Destynee said.

"It does not speak to us?" said Weems, astounded. "It does
not…speak?"

"I'm not an it!" Destynee shouted. "I'm a girl!"

"It is angry," Weems said.

"Of course it's angry!" Destynee shouted. "I mean- me."

"But from what cause?" said Weems. "It has given us no
reasons!"

"Maybe you should ask your girlfriend," said Destynee. "You
know, your Beloved."

Weems stopped and looked at her. He opened his mouth, and for
a moment, Destynee could see his tongue flicking behind his jagged
teeth. He raised his hands in the air and twiddled his fingers as if he
were plucking the strings of an invisible harp. "Perhaps— "he said.
"I have spoken words to cause you dismay."

"Perhaps I have spoken words to cause you dismay," said
Destynee. "Did anyone ever tell you what you sound like when you
talk? An idiot."

"It must not say such things," said Weems. "We did not mean
to cause this."

"Of course you did!" Destynee shouted, and stamped her foot.
Sewer-water splashed onto Weem's shirt. "You don't care about
me! You never have! You said that you liked me, that I was special
to you, and then the second another Giant Enchanted Slug comes
along, you're all over her. You don't love any one for who they are!

All you care about is that they're a Giant Enchanted Slug!" Her voice caught, and tears spilled over her lashes. As the tears rolled down, steam rose from Destynee's face.

"It must not cry," said Weems. "The salt… it will melt the face of the Beloved."

"I'm not the Beloved!" shouted Destynee. "That other slug is your Beloved. You said so!"

"My sweet— " said Weems. "Forgive me. I— I have a heart that is…perhaps pulled too easily toward the crunchy."

"Shut up," said Destynee. "Just shut up."

"Please," said Weems. "Forgive me. I did not see." He kneeled down in the waste water, and took her hand.

"I don't care if you're sorry," said Destynee. "It doesn't make any difference."

"What would make this difference then?" said Weems. "It must tell us. We wish to undo the hurt we have caused. Might I— might I roast something for you? We might eat the little bones of something!"

"I don't want to eat little bones!" said Destynee. "I just want you to see me for who I am!"

"But who is this!" said Weems. "Who is this that you are? Is it this girl? Or is it the sweet mollusk that lives within? I cannot see what you cannot show!"

"I'm both, okay?" said Destynee. "I'm me, and I'm a slug. It's the same thing."

"The same, it says," said Weems. "The same?"

"Yes," said Destynee. "If you're going to be my boyfriend, you have to go out with both of me."

"The… the boyfriend, it says?" said Weems. "It has never said it ever wanted us. All it has ever said is for us to go away. For so long it yearned for the Jonny instead."

"Because you don't love both parts of me."

"But— we do," said Weems. "Can you not see that? We just— We just do not know how to be with others. We only know one thing, and that is the roasting of crunchy things and eating of them. It is easier for me to be with the slug. Because it asks nothing of us."

"The slug side wants the same as the human side," said Destynee.

"And what is this? The crunchy bones?"

"No, you idiot!" shouted Destynee, and pushed Weems down into the trickle of sewage. "I want to be loved! Is that so hard to understand?"

Weems, on all fours, looked up at her like a beaten dog. "Yes," he said. "It is very hard."

"Well then," said Destynee, turning her back on the ghoul. "I don't see what there is to talk about."

"We did not say impossible," said Weems. "We said hard." He made a gurgling sound in his throat. "We do not know the language. No one has ever taught us. Capturing the little varmints and roasting their bones like drumsticks over a fire, that is what they taught us. We did not know that this was not enough."

"Oh no," said Destynee.

"But we are learning," said Weems. "We can be— better than we have been. We can, if she will guide us, be one who learns. We can be— we can be your ghoul-friend."

"No," said Destynee, more loudly. "Oh no, oh no."

"No?" said Weems. "This cannot be?"

"Weems," said Destynee. "Look." She pointed down the sewer in the direction from which they'd come, and now Weems understood why she'd been saying Oh no. It wasn't that she was refusing his love.

It was that the pulsing Slime was coming down the pipe toward them. It was glowing, and glowering, and gurgling. There was no way out. Soon it would be upon them, and Weems and Destynee would be sucked into its vibrating mass. Hawgh hawgh hawgh, it said. Pieces of other monsters it had absorbed and consumed surfaced for a moment within its churning form, then sank.

Destynee turned to Weems. "We're doomed," she said.

Weems got to his feet.

"Weems will save you," he said. "For now I see. I see you as one creature with many sides. All of whom I love."

"Wait, Weems—" said Destynee.

"Farewell," said Weems. And then he turned to face the slime.

•

Falcon followed the path through the dark woods. He only caught sight of Gunk once, on the path far ahead, and it was clear the boy was moving very swiftly. For the life of him, Falcon could not see why Gunk was running away from the school at such a speed, especially with all the parents gathered in the Cafetoriasium.

The path emerged in a clearing at the bottom of a hill. Something about this place was familiar. Falcon looked around the long green grass, at the ruins of a barn that stood just at the edge of the open space. Of course, Falcon thought. It's the Outpost, the place where the Bland-a-tron was hidden, the place where their mission had begun. It was in this very field that Mr. Hake had landed the Zeppelin last month. But why, Falcon thought, would Gunk be coming here?

He heard a shout, or a cry, from the barn, and Falcon rushed forward to find its source. Light flashed from the barn, and then was gone just as quickly. Now he heard music— gentle, soft harp music, like something you'd hear in a particularly sugary part of heaven.

Falcon entered the barn with his eye burning and his wings struggling against his back. For a moment he stood in the door of the barn, trying to understand what it was he was looking at. But the longer he stared, the more confused he felt.

Before him, flying through the air, was a tiny pink cherub, an overgrown baby with translucent wings. In one hand it held a wand with a star at its end. As it flew around the barn, it waved the wand, and sparkles fell in a shower from its tip. Wherever the sparkles fell, things changed into chocolate. There was a chocolate saddle and a chocolate pile of hay and a pair of chocolate buckets. In one corner, a fudgy Mr. Swishtail stood frozen behind a dark chocolate fence.

The cherub looked at Falcon, laughed either demonically or adorably, and then swept toward him. It raised its magic wand.

Falcon felt something explode within him. His wings burst out of his back, and ripped through his shirt. With a single pulse of his wings, Falcon rose into the air. The cherub shot its sparkles at him, but Falcon dodged the attack. "Tee-hee-hee," it said, and Falcon had just time to think, Tee-hee-hee? before a fireball burst out of his black eye, soared through the air and hit the cherub squarely in the chest. "Eeeee," it said, and spiraled toward the ground, where it crashed in a pile of chocolate hay.

"Waah, waah, waah," said the cherub, and pink tears began to pour down its cheeks. It held its magic wand up in the air. It was dented.

Falcon landed in the hay next to the cherub. "Gunk?" he said.

The cherub wiped its pink tears away. "I'm not Gunk any more."

"You're not?" said Falcon.

"I'm Twinkle. The little pink fairy."

Falcon thought about this. "Okay," he said.

"You're an angel, I guess?" said Twinkle. "Lucky you."

"Luck doesn't have anything to do with it," said Falcon, folding his wings down behind him now. "We are who we are."

"What's wrong with me?" said Twinkle. "I wanted to be the running back on the football team. Instead I'm a..." His voice fell. "Little pink fairy, I guess."

"Who says you can't be both?" said Falcon.

"What do you know about it?" said Twinkle. "You don't have the horrors come over you, like I do."

"The horrors?" said Falcon.

Twinkle looked at his wand. "I feel the spell coming on, and then I know I'm going to transform. I don't want to be a little pink fairy, okay? It's stupid."

"I'm sorry," said Falcon. "You don't get to choose what's in your core. You only get to choose what to do with it."

"Do?" said Twinkle. "You know what I do? I make chocolate. I wave this wand and I turn crap into chocolate. That's the deal." He handed Falcon some chewy caramel that lay by his side. "Here. Knock yourself out."

Falcon took the caramel from Twinkle and nodded somberly. He took a bite.

"Whoa," said Falcon.

"What?" said Twinkle, dejectedly.

"It's just— this is really good chocolate," said Falcon.

Twinkle looked up. "Really?" he said.

"Mr. Quinn. Mr. Gunkowski. What are you doing here?" said a voice, and they turned to see Mr. Connelly standing in the door of the barn, looking dark and angry. Falcon had never seen his teacher look quite so menacing before. Behind Mr. Connelly, holding baby Angelique, was Mrs. Connelly. She was as pale as curdled milk.

"I was trying to help," said Falcon. "I was trying to help, uh, Twinkle."

"Twinkle?" said Mr. Connelly. His face was turning red. "Who's Twinkle?"

But at this moment there was a rumbling from below their feet, and the floorboards of the old barn burst upwards and a huge arm of revolting slime erupted, like lava from an all-slime volcano.

"Hawgh hawgh hawgh," it said, as the slime spread into the barn. It raised its vibrating, gelatinous arms and stood there as if trying to decide whether it was Twinkle or Falcon, or the Connelly's, or all of them at once, that it would next destroy.

•

Tripper put his bucket down and stepped toward Pearl. "I warned you," he said. "Now you'll pay."

"And you," Pearl said, "shall feel the bite of cold steel! Ah, if only I were still in my monstrous form, then I could pierce you with my deadly poison! And you should regret the unkindness you have shown, to those whom I have pledged my honor!"

"Whatever," said Tripper. He reached into the bucket of manure and threw a handful at Pearl's face. He was a good shot, hitting her square in the face. Pearl was blinded by the poop that covered her now, and she fell onto the light bridge dropping the Sword of Damocles, which snapped beneath her.

"Later for you, Chupa," said Tripper, and looked down at the stage once more.

But Pearl's body, lying there on the bridge began to vibrate and pulse. She seemed to shrink in size. Two small wings, and then a long deadly stinger, appeared.

Pearl lifted her head and looked at Tripper once more.

"There shall be blood," she said.

•

On stage, the Bludstones had finished their performance of "Where Is Love," and everyone applauded wildly. Sparkbolt bowed, and Malcolm bowed, and Ankh-hoptet bowed, and Max bowed. A moment later, there was a shout from overhead.

Max looked up at the bridge where the lights for the stage were hung, and saw that there were people up there, and that they appeared to be fighting. He squinted, and then he thought he could see a little better— there was Tripper Murphy, holding what looked like a large bucket or a washtub, and there was Pearl— now fully transformed back into her Chupakabra form, buzzing around him.

"Uh-oh," said Max.

"You shall feel the poison of the stinger!" shouted Pearl. "You may blind me with poop! But you yourself are blinded by falsity! It is this that shall be your downfall! For your poop does not destroy my courage! My courage is stronger than poop yes it is!"

But Tripper was fast. He clapped his hands together suddenly, and the tiny Chupakabra was crushed between them. Once more she fell onto the bridge like a dragonfly that had been swatted.

"Ai!" said Pearl. "I am slain!"

"What are you, a talking bumblebee?" said Tripper. "Whatever you are, you're gross. And there's only one thing to do to things that are gross. "

He raised one foot to stomp on her.

Just then, another form appeared at the end of the lighting bridge, someone huge and menacing. Dark power seemed to radiate from the shadow. It stepped forward.

"Is Olga," she said.

Tripper, caught off guard, took a step backwards, and in doing so dropped his bucket of manure. It fell fifty feet below him onto the stage.

"You get back, you freak," said Tripper. "You don't belong here."

But Olga just laughed. She stepped forward, and lifted Tripper in one hand, and then threw him off the bridge. Tripper Murphy fell through the air, toward the stage, and then landed with one foot in the bucket of horse manure he had gathered with his own hands.

"Is not freak," said Olga. "Is Olga." Below her, Tripper Murphy struggled to get his foot out of the bucket, but he was firmly stuck, and Tripper clomped around the stage with his foot stuck in a bucket as the audience laughed uproariously. Olga nodded, then began to do a dance, there on the light bridge, the dance of the Large Maiden.

"My friend," said Pearl, buzzing toward her. "To you I am at last revealed!"

"Not revealed," said Olga. "Olga knew friend from start."

"And you—" said Pearl. "Are you as well a creature of imagination, hidden from all except those with eyes that see?"

Olga shrugged. "Comes from Vrzøzyz. Export is coal. Capital is Bharf." She smiled. "Olga lives in Bharf."

•

Back in the Barn, the Slime appeared taken off guard by the appearance of the Connellys, and now it oozed toward the back of the barn slightly, in the direction of the chocolatized Mr. Swishtail, as if to consider its options. There, to its right were Falcon and Gunk, or Twinkle, more properly, as the enormous, hairy running back remained transformed for the moment into his monstrous form of little pink fairy. But now, to its left, were Mr and Mrs. Connelly and their baby. The sheer abundance of beings whom it might slime next seemed to have given the creature an occasion to pause and think over its choices. Its protoplasmic arms waved gelatinously in the air.

The baby pointed at Twinkle, who, pink and swollen as he was, still appeared like an oversized, winged version of the baby itself. "Doomed," said Angelique.

The slime looked over at the baby and shook. Then it gurgled closer to the Connellys and oozed forward with a third arm, which it raised high above the little family as if to envelop them next with its vibrating jelly.

But now another group stormed through the door, and there in the straw stood Merideath and Judy Underhill, cleverly dressed up as a vampire and a zombie. As they entered the barn, their eyes grew wide and their mouths dropped open. Falcon could see Merideath's long canine teeth shining.

"Get back," said Mr. Connelly.

But the Slime seemed delighted to have yet more creatures to absorb, and it now extended a fourth arm in the direction of the newly-arrived young women and it raised its protoplasm in anticipation of striking them down.

"Falcon," said Mrs. Connelly, rushing forward with the baby in order to push Falcon down into the straw. At that same moment, one of the slimes bloblike arms came slapping down toward him. It would have absorbed him directly into its mass if Mrs. Connelly had not pushed him. The Slime made an angry rumbling sound, and it raised its arms again.

For a single second, the head of Jonny Frankenstein surfaced in the quivering scum, and then quickly sank again.

"This is intolerable," said Mr. Connelly.

"We shall stop it," said a voice, and now climbing out of the hole the Slime had burst through the floor, Weems stepped up into the barn. He held out one hand, and helped Destynee up.

"You cannot stop it," said Mrs. Connelly.

"You know about this slime?" said Falcon.

"Oh we know all about the slime," said Mrs. Connelly. "Believe me."

The baby pointed at Falcon and said, "Doomed."

The Slime extended another gelatinous arm and raised it above Destynee's head. But Weems stepped forward. "It shall not Slime the Beloved," he said.

"Somebody do something," said Judy Underhill.

"It cannot be stopped," said Mr. Connelly. "It just grows."

"I can stop disgusting slime," said Merideath. "Watch." She stepped forward and poked the slime with one of her long, pointy finger. "Hey you. Disgust-o. Show me what you've got."

The Slime gurgled for a moment, then reached out toward Merideath with one of its arms. But Merideath just grabbed the arm, raised it to her mouth and bit. The Slime vibrated for a moment, then howled with pain.

"Yuck," said Merideath. "That is the most disgusting thing I have ever bitten."

"Wait," said Destynee. "Did you just turn it into— vampire slime?"

"I did," said Merideath proudly.

"Um," said Destynee. "Was that a good idea?"

The Slime was still writhing and howling. It withdrew all of its arms into its mass and then flopped around the floor of the barn. A formation like a mouth rose up from within it, and a moment later, a creature none of them had ever seen before was spat out onto the straw. It was a frost worm. In one hand it held a copy of Catcher in the Rye.

"John," said Judy Underhill. "John McNinch?"

The frost worm shuddered and shrank, and a moment later a pale young man was sitting in its place. He shone with residual jelly. John McNinch looked over at the ailing slime and a look of terror crept over him again. "Don't let it get me," he said. "I don't want to go back."

But the Slime didn't seem as if it posed any immediate threat to John McNinch. It has turned a sickly green color, and as if writhed and vibrated, more things were spat out of its maw. A foot. Someone's arm. Muffy Chicago. And then, in a single piece, Dr. Frankenstein. He looked around the room, taking everyone in. "A zombie. A vampire. An angel. A ghoul. A giant enchanted slug. A little pink fairy. Yes, good."

"It has the weird-dar," explained Weems. "It can tell."

He picked up the foot that lay beside him. "Jonny," he said, excitedly. "My boy!"

The slime now spat out the other pieces of Jonny— his arms, his middle, and finally, his head. Dr. Frankenstein lifted the head into the air. "My son!" he shouted. "My precious son!"

"She bit the slime," said Twinkle. "She poisoned it."

The doctor, still shiny, looked from Jonny's head and over at the cherub. "Wait, what is this? The vampire bit the slime, you say?"

"I did," said Merideath proudly. "I drained its life force with the bite of Undying!"

"Oh no," said the doctor.

"Doctor, what is the matter?" said Mrs. Connelly.

"Don't you see," said Mr. Connelly. "She has not destroyed the slime. She has transformed it into Undead Slime."

"That's what I just said!" shouted Destynee.

Dr. Frankenstein looked at Mr. and Mrs. Connelly and their baby. "But what are these ones?" he said, his face growing more alarmed. "These ones are not known to me."

"I am," said Mr. Connelly. "The Crow."

As Falcon watched, the teacher transformed into the familiar figure of his father. There he was once more, the tall, gaunt man with the black wings.

"Wait, what?" said Falcon.

"Honey," said Mrs. Connelly, but as he turned to look at her she had already changed into his mother, Vega. The baby Angelique was still in her arms. "This is your sister."

"Doomed," said the baby.

"Hawgh-hawgh-hawgh," said a deep voice, and now the slime changed color, morphing from the sickly green to an angry, pulsing red. It rose up like lava, and reached out with two vibrating arms that instantly encircled Falcon's mother and father. They were raised, shouting, into the air, as a large mouth with long vampire teeth emerged in the center of the slime. The mouth opened wide, and the teeth shone. Then it began to lower The Crow and Vega and Baby Angelique towards its maw.

"We must stop it!" shouted the doctor. "If it bites them, they will become like it— masses of cruel undead protoplasm!"

"But how do we stop it?" said Destynee.

Falcon shot a fireball from his dark eye at the monster, but they just entered the slime's mass.

"Falcon," shouted Vega. "I'm sorry!"

The slime lowered Falcon's mother into its mouth.

"Oh for Petes sakes," said Twinkle, and flutered his wings. Just before the Slime's vampirous mouth clamped into Vega's body, the little pink fairy passed its dented wand over the creature's vibrating mass, and in an instant, the Slime transformed into chocolate. Twinkle circled around a couple more times, shaking his wand, but his work was already complete. The giant slime had been entirely changed into fudge.

"Someone..." said the Crow. "Get me down." He was trapped by the solid chocolate fingers of encircling, hardened slime.

Vega, less entombed, was able to step out of the chocolate mouth, her baby still in her arms, and brush herself off. "You'll have to eat yourself out, dear," she said.

"Wait," said Judy Underhill. One of her zombie eyeballs looked like it was just about to fall out of its socket. "Isn't that vampire chocolate now?"

"You say that like it's a bad thing," said Merideath.

"Yeah, hel-lo," said Destynee.

"Everyone's so critical," said Merideath.

"Mom? Dad?" said Falcon. "I don't understand. You've been—here all along?"

"Of course we have," said the Crow, still struggling to get out of the chocolate grip in which he was ensnared. "We have watched and guided your progress every day."

"Because we love you," said Vega.

"Doomed," said Angelique.

"You had a baby?" said Falcon.

Falcon's father managed to break off a piece of the chocolate and then squeezed out of the now-solid slime.

"My son," said the Crow, coming over to Falcon and putting his hand upon his shoulder. "Can you forgive us? After we left you—that day by the windmill— I had such work to nurse your mother to health. We had much to learn from each other, and much to forgive. We did not expect to have another child." He looked at Angelique. "But here she is. We were consumed with her. It was our desire to look out for you, to help undo the damage we have done. But then the mission began, and the baby was born, and all we could do was disguise ourselves, and look after you from a distance."

"Plus little Angelique is such a love-bucket," said Vega. The child growled. As Falcon watched, he saw that two small horns had begun to grow on either side of the baby's head. Its eyes glowed scarlet.

"I have a sister?" he said.

"Here," said Vega, handing Falcon the baby. "Hold her."

Falcon was not sure how to hold the baby, but he took her in his arms.

"Aw," said Merideath. "That's adora— buh, buh, buh—"

Destynee looked over at her. "Are you okay?"

"I'm fine," said Merideath, raising one hand to her head. "I just got a funny taste in my mouth."

"That is not slime," said Dr. Frankenstein.

"What does it say?" said Weems.

"That creature is not slime. It is something else."

"Well, it's chocolate now, isn't it?" said Destynee.

The doctor looked at Falcon. "You have a healing blue eye, do you not?"

"Yeah," said Falcon. "But how do you—"

"The hybrids always have the dual eyes. The dark one is a fireball? The blue one must be a healer."

Weems shook his head, impressed. "It knows much about the nature of things."

"Shine the light upon the creature," said the doctor. "And we will see what it truly is."

"I'll take the baby," said Vega, reaching out.

"Go on, son," said The Crow. "This task is for you."

Falcon concentrated, and the blue light shone from his eye and focused like a spotlight upon the slime. For a moment it just began to run, like melted chocolate, and then there was a bright flash, and everyone was blinded. Smoke drifted through the barn.

When the smoke cleared, there in the midst of the hay, where the Slime had been, was a tiny dog.

"Yap," said Yap.

"I suspected as much," said the doctor. "It is a transforming dog." He smiled. "Excellent! Excellent! All we have to do is teach the dog not to become the slime. It should be easy enough to teach this trick. It is not—it is not an old dog, I do not think?"

"Yap," said Yap, and looked around at its fellow monsters with a look of sorrow.

"You're a bad dog," said Twinkle, and pointed his dented wand at the little dog.

"Yap," said Yap.

"Whoa," said a voice from the door, and Max stepped into the barn, followed by a small crowd of others— Malcolm, Sparkbolt, Ankh-hoptet, Quacky, Olga, and Pearl.

Some of them were humans disguised as monsters for Halloween; others were monsters revealed as their true selves. Falcon, looking from face to face, could not immediately tell one from the other.

"Dude," said Max. "Looks like we missed something."

Olga looked around the room, at the Crow and Vega and Falcon and baby Angelique, the Crow's black wings gathered around his family; at Dr. Frankenstein holding the head of his son Jonny in one hand, staring into his boy's closed eyes; at Destynee and Weems, who were now drawing close together in a kiss.

Olga reached down to her side and raised the Horn of Vrzøzyz. She held it to her lips and blew. It was a sweet, musical note that filled all who heard it with a sense of hope, a sense of old woes being put to rest, and a time of new beginnings coming to pass at last.

"Has horn," said Olga.

12.

Falcon Quinn Spreads His Wings

"The only thing I like more than flying a Zeppelin," said Mr. Hake dreamily, "is bacon." For a moment, Mr. Hake, transported by the ecstasy of the very thought of bacon, morphed into the Terrible Kraken, and his tentacles erupted in every direction and his enormous wet eyes rolled around in his rubbery exoskeleton. Then, a moment later, he returned to his previous form, and there he was once more, mild mannered, wearing a cardigan sweater, a captain's hat upon his head.

"Mr. Hake, do know that we share your sense of joy," said Mrs. Redflint, as smoke slowly drifted from her nostrils. "But perhaps you should return to the controls?" She looked out upon the Atlantic Ocean, which stretched below them in all directions. "I fear that we might begin to drift."

"Oh, we are all righty-roo," said Mr. Hake contentedly. "I have a new co-pilot!" He waved toward the pilot-house at the front of the Zeppelin, where Ankh-hoptet was steering the dirigible with a look of extreme importance. She looked out over the horizon and nodded with an expression that seemed to say, At last I have found my kingdom.

"She knows our destination?" said Mrs. Redflint.

"Oh she does," said Mr. Hake. "It makes her happy-happy! Which is so much better than happy-unhappy! You see, happy-happy is when you are happy that you are happy. But happy-unhappy is when you are not happy, but you are happy about being unhappy. And that is so different from unhappy-happy, which is when being unhappy makes you—"

Mrs. Redflint sent a sudden blast of fire from her mouth in Mr. Hake's direction, and a moment later, the man's cheeks were covered in soot and his hair was singed and standing upright. "Ooh! Ooh!" he said, jumping up and down on one leg. "You gave me a hot foot, Mrs. Redflint!"

"Mr. Hake," said Mrs. Redflint. "I do not need all the forms of happiness and unhappiness described in full."

"So you are saying," said Mr. Hake. "That hearing about unhappy-happy and happy-unhappy makes you—"

"Don't," said Mrs. Redflint, thick smoke billowing from her nostrils once more. "Just don't."

"Seems like old times, man," said Max, looking at the Dean of Students and the Vice-Principal.

"Indeed!" said Pearl, buzzing around the Sasquatch's head. "Once more we have come together to honor our pledges to each other. As friends!"

"We have," said Falcon. He was in angel form once more, his wings out, his halo glowing softly above him. He looked at the newest members of the Academy for Monsters— Judy Underhill, John McNinch, Twinkle, and Muffy Chicago, all gathered by the blimp's railing, looking out over the sea. There they were: a zombie, a frost worm, a little pink fairy, and a giant enchanted slug, with the ocean breeze in their hair, the sun on their faces, with no more reason to live in hiding. In looking at that group, Falcon wished that everyone—monster or human—could know this same freedom.

Merideath stood by Muffy's side, pointing at something on the horizon. She had become very close to Muffy, and in spite of learning that the girl was a giant enchanted slug, rather than a vampire like herself, she had continued being her friend. This struck Falcon as a good sign, an indication perhaps that even Merideath was becoming more forgiving, or at least as forgiving as a vampire could be.

She looked up at Falcon for a moment and the two locked eyes. Falcon noticed that she seemed paler than usual, that there was a slightly greenish tint to her skin.

"You think Merideath is all right?" said Falcon.

"I don't know, man," said Max. "I think maybe that Slime might have gone down the wrong pipe."

"She was describing her condition this very day!" said Pearl. "In terms that might give one reason for alarm!"

"Maybe you should hit her with some of your wacky blue light, man," said Max to Falcon. "Nurse her back to health."

"I do not think it is the enduring taste of slime which has brought her to this state!" said Pearl. "It is I believe the condition of Senor Jonny, whose disassembly has pierced her very heart!" Pearl buzzed to the side of Falcon's head, and flew in and out of his halo. "Her feelings for Senor Jonny are powerful indeed!"

"I hope his Pop can, like, fix him up and stuff," said Max.

"I do, too," said Falcon.

"There!" said Pearl. "Even now, with scientific rigor and parental regard, Padre Frankenstein is focused entirely on returning our friend to us better than before!"

At a small desk inside the Zeppelin's lounge, Dr. Frankenstein was screwing Johnny's head back onto his body. Some wires plugged into the sockets in Jonny's neck ran into the USB port of a laptop computer. Jonny's arms rose and fell, the hands opening and closing. But his eyes did not open.

Just behind the scientist stood the man's other son, Sparkbolt, wearing an expression of extreme concern. "Rrr," he said.

Next to the laptop, sitting on the table, was the chocolatized form of Yap. Mrs. Redflint was insistent upon taking all the monsters back to the Academy. It was her hope that with some education, Yap's sense of self might be improved. In time, she felt, Yap might have more control over when he morphed into the horrible slime. In time she hoped that, when he did transmogrify, he would not feel compelled to sweep everyone into his blob.

"Education," Mrs. Redflint had pronounced. "The great equalizer! Even for Blobs!"

At the front of the Zeppelin, Weems and Destynee stood together, talking softly. Weems' small pale arm rested on Destynee's back. She laughed at something he said, and Weems laughed back. Standing there listening, it occurred to Falcon that he had never heard Weems laugh before.

Dr. Frankenstein typed away on the keyboard of the laptop, and for a moment, Jonny's eyes flashed open. "Eye eye eye eye," he said.

"Rrrar!" shouted Sparkbolt.

Then there was a short puff of smoke, and Jonny's eyes closed once more.

"It does not appear that Padre Frankenstein is making the progress which he desires!" said Pearl.

"He'll work it out, man," said Max. "He's just gotta upgrade him so he doesn't get all run down."

"I wish someone would upgrade me," muttered Falcon, looking out at the ocean.

"What is this?" said Pearl. "Falcon Quinn, expressing once more his thoughts of dismay?"

"I'm all right," said Falcon.

"Hey, you gotta share your feelings, man," said Max. "I mean, like, sometimes I just wanna go——-HEEYYYYY——-so loud!"

Mrs. Redflint covered her ears. "Maximillian," she said. "Please. There is no reason for shouting."

"Sure there is, Mrs. R," said Max. "Sometimes you just gotta roar, am I right? Sometimes you gotta get out there and go bouncing."

"Our Sasquatch friend feels many things in large measure," said Pearl. "But it may be that in smaller portions, there is truth in his words which many can share!"

"Yeah," said Max. "Exactly."

"I'm okay, really," said Falcon. "It's just— I miss Megan, you know? She flashed out and never came back. Plus— my parents. I know they're sorry and everything, for the way they've treated me. But I don't know. Sometimes I'm just still mad at them."

At the back of the observation deck, Falcon saw his parents and baby Angelique, gathered together. The Crow was bent over the swaddled baby, caressing its dimpled chin. Falcon had never seen an expression like this on his father's face before.

It occurred to Falcon that his parents, as old as they were, were at the beginning of an adventure, rather than at the end of one. In the years ahead, they would raise little Angelique, teach her to read and write, to ride a bike, and to destroy enemies with blasts of molten flame. She was part of a new story for them, whereas he, their son, was part of an older one. He wanted to feel happy for them, and he did. But he also still felt restless. He wished that when his father had looked at him, that he had seen, just once, an expression on The Crow's face like the one he had right now.

"Sometimes," Falcon said. "I feel like I should set out on my own."

"That's crazy talk, man," said Max. "You're messing with my head."

Falcon turned to face them. "Sometimes I think I should," he said.

"Senor," said Pearl. "These are not words to be spoken except in the tones most serious!"

"I mean—" Falcon said. "I learned a lot from the Academy. I found my parents, as messed-up as they are. I made the best friends I'll ever make in my life."

"In this gift you are not alone!" said Pearl.

"But I'm thinking there must be more," said Falcon. "Now that I know what I am, I think I have more work to do."

"And what is the nature of this work?" said Pearl.

"I have to be an angel," said Falcon. "I have to be an angel of change."

"Okay, look," said Max. "You're kind of bumming me out. This kind of talk is totatally wonkaly."

A forceful gust of wind from the Atlantic blew across the deck of the Zeppelin, and for a moment it caught in Falcon's wings and lifted him off his feet.

Pearl looked at Max. "I have not felt this wind," she said. "It seems, Senor Falcon, to blow upon you and you alone."

The three friends stood there for a moment, thinking.

Then Max said, "Dude. It's her."

Falcon felt his twin hearts beating.

"Listen," he said. "I think I'm in the mood to stretch my wings a little."

"Yeah why not," said Max. "Exercise is good for ya. It's one reason I've got so into bouncing. It's really good for your glutes."

"Senor Max," said Pearl. "I do not think you are grasping all that Senor Falcon intends."

"Yeah, whatever," said Max. "Wait, what?"

Falcon's wings were spread over his head, and another blast of wind raised him off his feet, and then set him down. Once more it appeared as if this gale blew for Falcon, and Falcon alone.

"I think Senor Falcon will be gone for a while," she said.

"No way," said Max. "After everything we been through? I was thinking maybe we could finally take a vacation."

"It's not a big deal," said Falcon, looking at his parents once more. Now his mother was singing softly to his sister. "I just think I ought to look around. See what else is out there."

"You're killin' me," said Max. "Are you listening? You're totally killin' me." He threw back his head and he roared.

"My friend," said Pearl. "I cannot say that I have felt the thing that you now feel. But our pledge shall not be broken. We shall be friends, forever! The loyalty of those who have pledged their swords and stingers together cannot be broken— by distance, or time, or even the cruel mysteries of this world!"

"You're killin' me," said Max.

The wind blew again, and Falcon was lifted off his feet once more. "Okay," he said. "I feel you. I know you're there."

"It is of Senorita Megan that you speak!" said Pearl. "This one has become the wind. But this wind she has become is strong in its love for you!"

"Wait," said Max, tears in his eyes. "Just wait."

Max went inside for a moment, leaving Falcon alone on the deck with Pearl. Inside, Dr. Frankenstein was clacking away at his computer. Sparkbolt stood at his fathers' side, looking on with concern.

"Rrr," he said.

"I think that in time you will forgive them, Senor," said Pearl softly.

"Who?" said Falcon.

"These ones who ought to have been beside you," said Pearl. "As they should have been." She looked over at the Crow and Vega. "But these too are only what they are. We do not love others because they never make mistakes. We love them because of these. Or so it seems to me, in the station of my birth."

"Your station," said Falcon. "You mean as La Chupakabra. The famous goatsucker of Peru."

"No, Senor," said Pearl. "I mean this as your friend. Who shall stand with my stinger ready to defend you, until the final day."

Falcon nodded. "You're all right, Pearl," he said. Another gust of wind lifted him into the air, and this time he pulsed his wings and he turned his back upon the Zeppelin.

"Say goodbye to Max for me, okay?" said Falcon. "I don't think he understands."

"In this you are wrong," said Pearl, who flew up to where Falcon was hovering. "Senor Max understands all things. But then, he can tell you himself."

"Dude," said a voice, and Falcon swept back toward the Zeppelin for a moment. Max was standing at the railing holding a styrofoam cup. "I got you some cocoa."

Falcon flew back to the blimp and reached out with one hand and took the cocoa from the Sasquatch.

"Our lives," said Max. "Are totally, unbelievably, great."

"Thanks, Max," said Falcon.

"And don't forget to bounce," said Max.

"Indeed," said Pearl, orbiting Max's head. "Farewell."

Falcon pulsed his wings a couple of times, and headed out to sea. His father, The Crow, lifted his head to watch him go, and a sad smile creased his lips. He remembered the first time Falcon had flown up to his Tower at the Academy, how his son had helped set him free.

"Look, honey," said Vega, adoring little Angelique. "She's smiling!"

In the parlor, Dr Frankenstein entered another string of numbers into the keyboard, and then hit ENTER. There was a buzzing,

electrical sound, and suddenly Jonny's eyes opened. "Eye eye eye,"
he said, and looked around. He blinked, then raised one hand to his
forehead. "I've been— where am I?"

"Here," said Sparkbolt. "Brother. Father. Family. Safe."

"Wait," said Jonny. "Where's Falcon? I have to tell him
something."

Sparkbolt looked through the parlors glass windows and saw
Falcon soaring out above the sea. "Friend gone," he said sadly.

"But I need to tell him," said Jonny. "He's in danger. Terrible
danger. He doesn't know. I saw him. In my dream. I saw him!"

"Now now now, son," said Dr. Frankenstein. "You've been
offline for a long time. All sorts of data is corrupted on your hard
drive. You just need to relax a little while we de-bug you."

"Falcon," Jonny said, but the light was slowly dying from his
eyes now. "Falcon..." he whispered.

"Him losing power," said Sparkbolt. "Fix brother!"

"Fah—" said Jonny, and then his features froze.

"Oh, look at that, he's crashed again," said the doctor. He
looked at Sparkbolt, whose face showed sadness, as if he'd just lost
his best friend.

"Bad," said Sparkbolt.

"Oh, we'll get him up and running," said Dr. Frankenstein.
"We're almost there. Then I'll upgrade you too, Sparky! We need
to program some higher grammar functions into you. Give you

some foreign languages. Wouldn't you like to know French and German? How about ancient Greek?"

But Sparkbolt just looked through the window at the receding form of Falcon Quinn.

"Friend," he said, as if it were the only word Sparkbolt would ever know, and the only word he would ever need.

Out above the Atlantic, Falcon felt the sun on his face. He understood now that in the years to come, he and Megan would be one, that he would spread his wings and that she, the spirit of the wind, would lift him skyward.

Falcon did not know what adventures lay before him, or whether he would ever see any of his friends again. But he knew that he had become himself in part because of their loyalty, and their love.

He tasted the cocoa that Max had given him, and smiled. It was good. He pulsed his wings and rose.

About the Author

Jennifer Finney Boylan is the author of fourteen books, including a bestselling memoir, a collection of short stories entitled *Remind Me to Murder You Later*, six novels for young adults, and three novels for adults. She is the Writer-in-Residence at Barnard College of Columbia University.

Jenny Boylan lives at the end of a dirt road in Maine with a Sasquatch, a wind elemental, two were dogs, and a leprechaun. To learn more about Jenny and Falcon and to find a wide range of bonus material for this series, visit www.falconquinn.com.

The writing of this book was made possible by a grant from the Comer Family Foundation. For more information on the Foundation, please visit comerfamilyfoundation.org. Proceeds from the sales of this book go to benefit the anti-bullying initiatives of GLAAD, the media advocacy nonprofit for worldwide civil rights. Please visit www.glaad.org for more about their work.

Readers may write the author at quimby@falconquinn.com.